COLUMBARIUM

CONDEMNED SOULS

ANGELA DUNGEE-FARLEY

ISBN: 1477508317
ISBN 13: 9781477508312

To everyone who read my two previously published books,
this book, and to those who will read my future books…
I thank you.

CONTENTS

ACKNOWLEDGMENT

The great composer J.S. Bach
His many wonderful compositions,
were constant companions during countless
hours of writing.

CAST OF CHARACTERS

Father Demetric   Missionary priest, leader

Bishop Fabius   Church first bishop

Father Augustus   Roman Catholic priest

Leslie Lovette, PhD   Instructor, Graduate
                           Architect Program with a
                           passion for historic sites,
                           preservationist

Justine Coates   Student, Architect
                           Program, brainy, en-
                           vironmentalist, strong
                           preservationist

Damian Lovecraft   Student, Architect
                           Program, arrogant, crude,
                           comes from old money

Kyle Quentin	Student, Architect Program, jokester, wants to fit in
Josh Morrow	Student, Architect Program, always up for an adventure, a "wanna-be-explorer"
Samantha Prentiss	Student, Architect Program, attractive, flirty, feels her looks will get her everything and everywhere
Warren Sykes	Student, Architect Program, smart, hard worker, struggles financially
Alexandria Haigler, PhD	Director of Graduate Studies, Architect Program
Archbishop	Local archdiocese
Father Vita	Catholic Priest
Bishop Quintus	Performs deconsecration
John Lucianus	Church rector

Sebastian	Church handyman/ groundskeeper
Jeff Midtomac	Renowned photojournalist

PREFACE

The author wishes to convey to the reader that *Columbarium, Condemned Souls* is purely a fictional piece of work. It was written to entertain and to frighten; it is not intended to mislead, offend or conflict. Certain dates, events, ceremonial rites, and historical facts have been altered, as a means of suspense. They are not intended to challenge or oppose historical facts or religious beliefs, as we know them to be. This book is an indulgence for the imagination, from the mind of a fictional horror writer, who absolutely adores the genre and wishes to share this experience with each and every one of you.

SCENE 1: THE BEGINNING

The year was 1780, and the war between Spain and France over control of Italy continued. It was a war that had begun around the mid-fifteenth century and had no end in sight. The unrest was relentless, the loss of human life horrifying, and for many, the notion of continuing under these conditions was unbearable. So a group of Roman Catholics from a small city on the outskirts of Rome, led by a young missionary priest named Father Demetric, decided to migrate to a new world, a world known as America. This America was a place of new freedoms, new opportunities, and new beginnings unheard of in their motherland. Father Demetric and his followers were the first Roman Catholics to travel to this new land, long before any recorded migrations from their motherland…Italy.

The journey was long and hard, and some didn't make it, but the others pushed on. They left behind neighbors, family, and friends, traveling with only bare bones, and were only allowed to carry a small memento, such as a ring, book or coin, some token or remembrance of those left behind—that is, with the exception of the materials needed to build their dream church upon arrival to this new world. Therefore, the followers had to make financial sacrifices in order to do God's work. The parting of all worldly possessions, even treasured and coveted family possessions for the greater good… this was Father Demetric's creed. According to Father Demetric, these sacrifices were imperative if they were to make their dream a reality once in America. This meant prior to leaving Rome, everyone partaking in the journey had to sell any and all personal belongings with any financial value. This was no sacrifice and was very much worth it to this group of devout Catholics. The money would allow them an opportunity to acquire the materials needed to create a structure that would rival that in their motherland.

They journeyed to this new world with all the ornamentations and adornments needed to create their house of worship, such as moldings, tiles, frescoes, mosaics, and stained glass for custom windows. But their most beloved and valued treasure of all was a "Holy Tabernacle," which housed the Blessed Sacrament/Eucharist. It is said to have been blessed by a saint from their region, a gift for their journey to this new land. It was a masterpiece made of solid bronze. It was not very large in size but an extremely weighted piece, requiring two to three men to move it about safely, a marvel for the eyes to see. It would be the focal point near the altar for all to see and adore, a beacon that would call to its parishioners for Sunday services and daily Mass. It was both the link to their past and the lantern to their future. Upon arrival to this new land in 1781, they colonized an area known as Hudson Valley, New York. The Indians called their location Sleepwater. They would be the first Roman Catholics to this area, though history would have you believe otherwise. But they were not the first immigrants to journey to this Hudson Valley, quite the contrary; that would have been the Dutch and the French.

Once settled, three years later the colony began building their church, a cathedral, under the disciplined leadership of Father Demetric. Many of the men working to build the church were master craftsmen in their native Italy, men who took pride in their work, who were meticulous, and who labored well under pressure. The year was 1789, and after five years of hard labor under the rigid guidance of Father Demetric, the church was completed...and what a vision. "The Church of all Saints" it was named, a cathedral, and though slightly smaller in stature than those found in Italy, it was no less divine.

The day for the consecration of the new church had arrived, which meant all were expected to attend... as per Father Demetric...no exceptions. The parishioners gathered on the outside of the church awaiting their cue to enter. The exterior was a masterpiece, and when the doors opened to reveal the church's interior, it was more than their eyes could behold; it was vision. It presented with the three-aisled interior, compound piers and rib vaults and, amazing stain glass windows.

A version of what would have been found in Rome, just slightly smaller, but a giant in its own right. The parishioners were in amazement as they entered the building, but the best was yet to come.

Once in the church and seated, the parishioners turn their attention to the altar, where Father Demetric entered from an adjacent room, accompanied by the newly appointed rector. Bishop Fabius, who had traveled to this new land with the others, was there to perform the consecration. But shortly after the ceremony, a few months later, the bishop passed away, and since he was their only bishop, the responsibility was left to Father Demetric to lead the congregation. This day had been years in the making and is the final chapter of their journey to this new world. The weight of the Holy Tabernacle required the assistance of two male parishioners to lift it and place it atop a column, specifically designed for it near the altar. This is because the Holy Tabernacle housing the Blessed Sacrament/Eucharist was not allowed to rest on the main altar. It was placed on a raised column adjacent to the altar, where it was permanently affixed, while maintaining a line of vision for Father Demetric to the congregation. All were seated, and Bishop Fabius proceeded with the consecration ceremony. Once consecrated, all within the church was hallowed and blessed, and it became a sacred place. As Bishop Fabius was performing the consecration ceremony, an air of splendor and peace consumed the building. What appeared to have been an ordinary overcast day suddenly burst with sunshine, which poured through the stained glass windows and was taken as a sign of goodwill and prosperity ahead.

As time passed, all was good. A school had been built for the children, farming and harvesting was going well, merchants were selling and trading, the colony was blossoming, and there had been many births since they first colonized this new land. And in 1790 many more Roman Catholics migrated here from their motherland. The community was indeed thriving. But as the years pushed on, Father Demetric's dominance began to shift, and many of the decisions he made appeared to be ominous. His tolerance for human error began to weaken, as did his compassion, and eventually his stern rule turned to cruelty. When parishioners sinned and sought forgiveness during confession, he would decide whether or not they were entitled to redemption. Many were denied, and all too often the prayers required for redemption for a particular sin were withheld. Those who no longer followed his ways, those who had disembarked from the church, and even the crippled and those physically or emotionally too impaired to attend, were denied last rites upon dying. Father Demetric found them to be unworthy. Among others were stillborns and small children born out of wedlock, because according to Father Demetric, every child born out of wedlock is born from a whore's womb. They, too, were denied last rites and a burial on consecrated ground. Sinners of crimes such as murder, prostitution, rape, homosexuality, fornication, and insanity to name a few were all considered the most heinous, all unworthy. Father Demetric was both judge and juror, anyone seeking to get to heaven had to go through him. Many had to be buried secretly, in graves with other bodies, or on areas of consecrated ground that were unkempt, gravesites where Father Demetric was unlikely to travel. But that was not the end of his tyranny; his most horrific crime was yet to be revealed. During the construction of the church, unbeknownst to all except the builders, Father Demetric commissioned the workers to build a room at the sublevel of the church (below the basement), and its existence was not to be a noted in the official church blueprints. During this period it was not uncommon to have such a room, so to obey Father Demetric's request was not a concern for the builders.

A known whore in the community, whom the years had ravaged with the consequences of syphilis and madness, had wilted away and died in the asylum that Father Demetric had commissioned. There was no family and no one to claim the body, and if there had been, they dared not step forward from the shame of it all. The asylum looked to the church for a resolution. All the others over the years had been claimed by family or someone willing to bury the body among their own, but not this one.

Father Demetric was outraged; he was not going to allow a woman of ill repute, an impure, a common whore with a condemned soul, to be buried in the church cemetery. Then it came to him, the most monstrous of all his undertakings yet. He led five of his most trusted followers to the secret sublevel of the church and instructed them to build a columbarium within the wall. This columbarium would be the final resting place for souls not worthy of consecrated ground. In their motherland, Roman columbaria were built underground, so this was the perfect location for his sinister plan. They obeyed his command, and a *"Wall of the Damned,"* as he referred to it, was constructed to house the souls of the condemned, once cremated. The year was 1804 and although cremation was common practice in other parts of the world, it was not yet popular in this country. Father Demetric commissioned an oven that could reach the required temperatures to leave nothing but ashes, and housed it in the sanatorium/asylum, where the cremations were to be performed. The furnace was quite simple. The interior was constructed of fired clay and housed an iron crib used for lifting the bodies into the furnace. The furnace exterior was constructed of brick with a metal door with a small opening for observing. It is said that Father Demetric rarely missed a viewing. Following the cremation of "the unholy," as Father Demetric referred to them, the ashes were put into urns and placed in niches within the columbarium wall. The whore was the first to be placed in this wall, but many more followed. Each niche had a faceplate affixed to it with number, date, and name.

FATHER DEMETRIC

Here in this unconsecrated wall lies the remains of evil, may their souls never wander this earth again.

It became Father Demetric's passion to ensure that every unworthy soul became a part of this wall. There was also a book with the names of the condemned along with the niche number, date, and alleged crime(s) each soul was accused of committing. Now the year was 1824, and for twenty years Father Demetric's insolent behavior had been tolerated.

But the years had passed, and Father Demetric, a man of advanced age, had now sunken into madness, unable to care for himself. Because of his past actions, now considered crimes against humanity, he became a resident at the same asylum where so many had perished. He would reside there for the rest of his natural life, the very place he had condemned so many to... some still there.

The stench of decay filled the crematorium. The years of hell echoed through the walls where Father Demetric seemed to be a perfect fit. Surrounded by madness, grief, and despair, Father Demetric was too far gone mentally to even realize that he was now one of the condemned. After years of being locked away, Father Demetric passed away, and it is said that when his remains were placed on the iron crib and went through

the flames, it sent such a stench through the crematorium never before smelled. An odor that reeked of the
weeping, suffering, and pain consumed by those not
granted salvation. During the years Father Demetric
dwelled in the hell he had condemned so many to, no
one had been buried in the "Wall of the Damned."
Until now. The new priest, Father Augustus, and
his faithful servants journeyed to the sublevel, where
the wall still stood. There appeared to be hundreds
of niches, all unblessed souls Father Demetric had
condemned.

FATHER AUGUSTUS

*No one has entered this room or been entombed
in this wall since Father Demetric's tyranny. It
has remained locked and concealed. This is a
place of evil, and once Father Demetric's remains
are placed here, it will be concealed forever.*

Father Augustus's followers placed Father Demetric's
ashes into an urn and placed it within a niche, along-
side those he had condemned to this unconsecrated
wall years prior. On the faceplate was the number
(413), date (1829), and name (Father Demetric).
Father Augustus took the book and placed Father
Demetric's name in it along with the number, date,
and his crimes/sins.

FATHER AUGUSTUS

"This is the last entry to ever be placed in this book, so help us God.

He said a prayer for the lost souls then turned to one of his faithful followers, handing the book to him.

FATHER AUGUSTUS

"To you, my son, I bestow this book. I hereby name thee "Keeper of the Souls." You are charged with ensuring that these unhallowed souls remain in this wall for all eternity. This book is to be passed down throughout the years to your son and his son after, and his son after him…And may God travel with you through this journey".

The humble follower accepted the book and held it close. Upon exiting the room, the door was locked and sealed for all eternity.

SCENE 2: PRESENT DAY

The beautiful and vivacious Leslie Lovette, PhD stands in front of a very large and packed auditorium, delivering a lecture to her graduate students in architecture. The lecture is on two very important architectural design elements that contributed to the unique creation of an eighteenth-century Roman Catholic Church, located in Hudson Valley, New York. The two design elements are Roman Catholic and Gothic. As Dr. Lovette presents the slides on the projector, she shares pertinent information with the audience.

DR. LOVETTE

As you can see in these slides, some of the details of the church are prime examples of Charles Borromeo's Instructiones Fabricae et Supellectilis Ecclesiasticae, simply referred to as the Instructiones. As you may know, Borromeo was the cardinal archbishop of Milan. He is recognized as a saint in the Catholic religion. His Roman Catholic elements were combined with the elements of

Gothic design inspired by the Santa Maria Sopra Minerva, translation, Saint Mary Above Minerva, located in Rome, Italy, in the Piazza Della Minerva, within the ancient district. The two inspirations combined created this magnificent eighteenth-century Roman Catholic church. Though considered slightly smaller when it was built, in comparison to the churches found in Rome, this church takes up space comparable to two large city blocks. It is suggested but not officially recorded that The Church of All Saints is the first Roman Catholic church built in the Hudson Valley area, but this fact has been disputed by many, including the diocese.

She has a captive audience.

DR. LOVETTE

Notice the large square-projecting tower, which is the focal point of the church and dominates the façade. This type of tower is eighteenth- and early nineteenth- century tradition and not medieval precedent, as one might think. Charles Borromeo paid special attention to a church's exterior, which provides the Roman influence on this one. He felt the exterior of a structure should be visually prominent and that this theory applies especially to the entrance of churches in particular.

She now moves to the church's interior.

DR. LOVETTE

Here in the interior, you will notice the Santa Maria Sopra Minerva's Gothic detail inspiration on the interior, displaying its three-aisle design, with compound pier and rib vaults. These two styles when combined produced a masterpiece unlike anything ever seen before in that area.

Dr. Lovette looks up at the clock and notices it's time for the session to end.

DR. LOVETTE

OK, our time together for today is up. We can pick up from here next week. Enjoy your weekend and review everything we covered this week; there just might be a quiz on Monday.

The students start moving about collecting their belongings, to leave the room.

DR. LOVETTE

Oh…hold on for a minute.

Everyone stops.

DR. LOVETTE

If I call your name, please stay behind.

She picks up a sheet of paper and calls out the names.

DR. LOVETTE

Justine Coates, Josh Morrow, Samantha Prentiss, Damian Lovecraft, Warren Sykes, and Kyle Quentin. If I called your name, please come down and take a seat in the first row here.

The six students whose names she called join her as requested.

DR. LOVETTE

Thank you. As not only first-semester second-year graduate students in this program, you are also my brightest.

They look at one another with proud smiles.

DR. LOVETTE

As you may or may not be aware, from time to time I take the liberty…with the school's consent of course, of taking a few of my second-year students on a little field trip, a little adventure, if you will. Now something else you may or may not be aware of is…

She points to the slide with the picture of The Church of all Saints, the one whose architectural elements she has just reviewed with the class.

DR. LOVETTE

As mentioned, this is The Church of All Saints, located in Hudson Valley, completed in 1789. This church is slated for demolition, which is a crime in itself, since it is said to be the first Roman Catholic church built in that area, a fact never officially documented, not even by the diocese.

The students are in awe at what most architecture students and established architects would consider a grave injustice, particularly those who feel strongly about conservation…and that would be all of the students to some degree, with the exception of Damian Lovecraft. Mr. Lovecraft's take on architecture is "out with the old and in with the new."

DAMIAN LOVECRAFT

Well, there's no place in today's society for relics. The architects of today have to take their place in society, designing structures that represent today and tomorrow. It's time to give the past to yesterday and start building today for tomorrow.

Justine Coates, a self-appointed conservationist of any and all structures built prior to the twentieth century, is outraged.

JUSTINE COATES

You know, Lovecraft, if that's really what your name is...

The other students find her comment amusing.

JUSTINE COATES

It's people like you who can only see the bottom line. That structure is a testament to the past. You have no respect for those who paved the way for the rest of us. Why are you in this class anyway?

DAMIAN LOVECRAFT

Requirement!

Dr. Lovette interjects.

DR. LOVETTE

OK, everyone, you're all entitled to your own opinions, but since this class is a requirement, so is this trip...Unofficially.

Damian frowns, and Justine smirks at him.

DR. LOVETTE

Besides, architecture is not simply about what's old and what's new. It's also about the environment and what impacts it.

Justine interrupts, feeling the need to do so, since she's such a strong environmental advocate.

JUSTINE COATES

That's right. Tell him, Doctor!

Dr. Lovette continues.

DR. LOVETTE

It's also about sustainability, the environment, and communities, to name a few. Me, personally, yes, I'm a big advocate for the preservation of historical structures, churches in particular. I love to explore them, study them, and whenever possible, do my part to help ensure their existence for as long as possible, which includes, but is not limited to, a little protesting, lobbying, letter writing, etc…but all within the law.

Kyle Quentin chimes in, desperately wanting to be the teacher's pet.

KYLE QUENTIN

I heard somewhere you're quite the "Indiana Jones" of architecture, traveling the globe, preserving all things old…

He catches himself and stops talking feeling embarrassed, as his classmates roll their eyes and shake their heads.

Dr. Lovette smiles and responds.

DR. LOVETTE

Well, yes, as I said, it's no mystery that my first passion is that of historical architecture of the sixteenth, seventeenth, eighteenth, and even nineteenth centuries, and yes, particularly churches and their preservation above all, whenever possible. I love getting into churches deemed for demolition before they are destroyed, because it allows an opportunity to venture into areas with previously limited access or those that simply don't allow entrance. I feel it is an honor to be one of the last people to walk through a church that's a couple hundred years old, before it truly becomes a part of history. Sort of like going in under the radar, perhaps acquiring something long forgotten that can be shared with the rest of the world, because once the trucks and the dozers and every other heavy piece of machinery hits it...that's it.

Josh Morrow jumps in, self-proclaimed expeditionary and adventure seeker.

JOSH MORROW

Now you're talking my language, Doc. Finders keepers, all others just weep.

Dr. Lovette smiles and she continues.

DR. LOVETTE

These expeditions, if that's what you'd like to call them, are no different than those of, say, an archeologist. If there is something found that seems remotely valuable, or there is question of its value, it is going to be turned over to the university, they can battle it out with whomever, to establish whom it belongs to... the previous owners or the new owners.

Then Samantha Prentiss, class diva, chimes in with her opinion.

SAMANTHA PRENTISS

Well, if it's a beautiful piece of jewelry and I come across it, let's just say…I'm not making any promises.

The other classmates offer their thoughts on Samantha's comment. She just laughs and enjoys the attention as well as the opposition of others. All of the students, with the exception of Warren Sykes, express their views concerning the world of architecture and their upcoming field trip.

DR. LOVETTE

OK, a few logistics to go over before we go. I never take my students on trips without the consent of the university and the legal own-er of the structure we're going to tour. I have forms for you to sign (she holds them out) stating that the university is not responsible for any mishaps that could occur on this trip. No signature, no trip.

She points to the church still on the projector.

DR. LOVETTE

The Church of all Saints has been sold to a contractor and is slated for demo. It's pretty much a done deal, but luckily for us, not all the final papers have been signed, so until the new owners officially take over, which will happen Monday morning, the diocese has granted us permission to go in and study the architectural structure, etc., a privilege that may not be granted once the new owners takeover. To say that destroying this church is a waste and a crime to a historical structure is an understatement. But we do not have a say, But what we can do is look at this as an opportunity to learn and perhaps someday recreate the wondrous appeal of this very unique structure that's about to be destroyed. So who's on board?

There's enthusiasm from the group, with the exception of Damian, and Warren Sykes, who's still really quiet.

Damian Lovecraft rolls his eyes, sighs, and looks up at the ceiling.

DR. LOVETTE

OK, go home, get some rest, and I'll meet you back here early Sunday morning at 9:00 a.m. We'll be taking one of the university's minivans. I'll be driving, so be here on time. Bring

*supplies needed such as a pen, pad, comput-
er...and an open mind; this just might turn
out to be the adventure of a lifetime. OK, see
you Sunday.*

The students are leaving the lecture hall.

DR. LOVETTE

*Mr. Sykes, could you stay behind for a min-
ute? I'd like to speak with you.*

He gestures, indicating yes. All the other students
exit the lecture hall.

DR. LOVETTE

Mr. Sykes...

He smiles.

WARREN SYKES

Warren, please...if you don't mind.

DR. LOVETTE

*OK, Warren...I couldn't help but notice that
you were very quiet and didn't voice an opinion one way or the other concerning our little
road trip.*

She looks down at a sheet of paper lying on the table right behind her.

DR. LOVETTE

I see here that you're a very attentive student in all of your classes and not just this one. But you tend to be standoffish and somewhat of a loner when assigned group assignments, such as colloquiums…that is, according to your graduate advisor.

He does not respond.

DR. LOVETTE

I also see here that there are some financial issues that might hinder your abilities to complete this program, which would be very sad because I believe that with your academic performance you could become a successful architect. But it's going to take more than book smarts to make it in this business…it's going to take being able to work with others regardless of personal issues.

He's still very quiet and only listens.

DR. LOVETTE

So will you be joining us on Sunday?

He smiles and nods, indicating yes.

DR. LOVETTE

OK, so we'll see you on Sunday.

Warren exits the lecture hall, as Dr. Alexandria Haigler, Program Director, enters. Dr. Haigler, a tall, trim, attractive woman in her midfifties, with an obvious discerning taste for the finer things in life, enters the room in designer apparel. An architect by trade, but very hands-off, she prefers administrative duties to fieldwork.

DR. HAIGLER

OK, I see you have your next group of very enthusiastic and eager participants geared and ready to partake on another of your interactive field trips.

Dr. Lovette jokingly responds.

DR. LOVETTE

There's always room for one more.

They both smile.

DR. LOVETTE

Make fun all you want, but this just might be the adventure of a lifetime for this group… that is until they're out in the working world. Remember that age and how excited you were just thinking about traveling the world, exploring different lands and landmarks and their architecture, even their ruins…oh my, I so love ruins.

DR. HAIGLER

Are you sure you're an architect?

Dr. Lovette appears baffled by Dr. Haigler's comment.

DR. LOVETTE

Excuse me?

DR. HAIGLER

Are you sure you're not secretly an archeologist, with all the exploring and excavating.

Dr. Lovette simply smiles.

DR. LOVETTE

I never excavate; I just...examine. Alex, you don't miss being out in the field, getting your hands dirty, and exposing architectural details lost in time? And the artwork on the stained glass windows just takes you to another place, another time.

Dr. Haigler places her hand on Dr. Lovett's shoulder.

DR. HAIGLER

No thanks, I'm pretty grounded right here, in the present, and it's where I prefer to be. Anyway, I lost that "virginality" a long time ago. I think I just made up a new word. Besides, I'd rather live vicariously through your adventures with your students. Leslie, I don't understand you. You were at the top of our class, both academically and creatively. With your knowledge and skills in architecture, you would have owned this city. Every firm from New York to Chicago wanted you...but you chose this. I can't understand.

DR. LOVETTE

I can't help it if I love historical sites, with their mosaics, frescoes, and pillows, as opposed to straight lines found in most modern architecture. This is where I belong. Believe it or not, I'm happy wandering through past centuries.

They both laugh.

DR. HAIGLER

Let me get out of your way so that you can get out of here and rest for your big adventure.

DR. LOVETTE

Well, if you change your mind and decide to join us, there's plenty of room in the van.

Dr. Haigler, walks away waving her hand in the air.

DR. HAIGLER

I won't.

Dr. Lovette smiles and continues collecting her belongings, then exits the lecture hall.

SCENE 3: SATURDAY MORNING MEETING AT THE CHURCH OF ALL SAINTS

A meeting is being held at The Church of All Saints between the archbishop, resident priest Father Vita, Bishop Quintus, and the church rector John Lucianus, concerning the selling and closing of the church. The archbishop is positioned at the altar, occupying Father Vita's seat while breaking the unpleasant but expected news concerning the church's future.

ARCHBISHOP

Well, the news I'm about to deliver to you should not come as a shock. For several years now, The Church of All Saints has been... for lack of better words, a "financial burden," one that the archdiocese can no longer afford to carry.

Father Vita humbly interjects.

FATHER VITA

But your Excellency, The Church of All Saints, as you know, has been a beckon in the community of Sleepwater since 1789...and being the first Roman Catholic church built in this area...well, your Excellency, by all rights it really should be deemed a historic institution with preservation status...sir. And might I be allowed to add that the parishioners not only attend Sunday services but Mass throughout the week. These are hardworking Christian families, most of whom have been raised in The Church of All Saints, and let's not forget, this is a strong Roman Catholic community. With all due respect, your Excellency, I feel that I speak for most if not all when I say that they are not pleased. In fact, that's an understatement, especially for those who fought so hard for the church not to be closed.

The archbishop responds.

ARCHBISHOP

That is all good and well, but desperate times call for desperate measures. And as for those outspoken opposers who insist that the church is being closed for financial gain, just because the church is being sold to a development company...well, that could not be farther from the truth. With the cost of upkeep, repairs, utilities, and a litany of other expenses, it is impossible to keep it open. It is unfortunate, but closing is the only practical thing to do. The closing of churches across the country seems to be the trend...churches of all denominations, not just Roman Catholic. We should be counting our blessings that we have a buyer willing to buy at market price and not below, considering the hardships the economy has been experiencing over the years. As for the parishioners who have been attending The Church of All Saints, who are now concerned as to where they will be able to worship, well, as you know, two counties over, about twenty miles away, is Saint Matthews. Their congregation is a modest size, so with the addition of your parishioners, they should have a full congregation. And as for The Church of All Saints being the first Roman Catholic church in this area, well, that's never been proven. The diocese respects the date printed on the church...but that too is questionable.

There's silence.

ARCHBISHOP

With that said, I hold in my hand a "decree"
which states that this church has been relegat-
ed to "profane use."

Immediately following this statement, Sebastian, the
groundskeeper and handyman, interrupts the meeting. Sebastian has always been a part of The Church of
All Saints, holding the same position his father held,
his father before him, and his father before him. He is
obviously upset and agitated in response to the official
notice of the church's closing.

SEBASTIAN

"Profane use?" You speak of "profane use"…
What's wrong with you people? By closing
the church, do you realize what will happen
to all of us?

The archbishop reacts.

ARCHBISHOP

Who is this person?

Father Vita hurries off the altar down to the Sebastian.

FATHER VITA

Come. You must come with me.

Father Vita addresses the archbishop.

FATHER VITA

This is Sebastian; he's our groundskeeper and handyman. He has not been not been himself lately...an illness.

SEBASTIAN

I do not stand here as a result of sickness but as a warning that if this church is to be closed, nothing good will come of it. It is the residents of Sleepwater who will pay the price.

FATHER VITA

Sebastian has very strong superstitious beliefs and is very passionate of the old ways. He has been brought up on myths and legends his entire life, passed down through the generations from his father and his father before him. I assure you he means no disrespect.

The archbishop attempts to lecture to Sebastian on the undisputed facts.

ARCHBISHOP

It is the decision of the diocese that this church be sold.

Sebastian interrupts again.

SEBASTIAN

The decision of the diocese? With all due respect, The Church of All Saints was standing long before there was even a diocese in this country.

ARCHBISHOP

That remains to be proven, and it is quite obvious that you oppose this decision, but a decision has been made and will be carried through. Tomorrow morning following Mass, Bishop Quintus, you will perform the deconsecration ceremony of The Church of All Saints.

SEBASTIAN

Please, I beg of you…To try and close The Church of All Saints will be a grave mistake that we will indeed regret.

Father Vita consoles Sebastian.

FATHER VITA

Come, Sebastian, I will take care of you.

Sebastian appears calmer.

FATHER VITA

Please, Your Excellency, might I be excused to console and pray with this weary soul?

The archbishop gestures with his hand, excusing Father Vita to leave. Father Vita leaves, comforting Sebastian, who appears exhausted, second to worrying and a troubled and heavy heart.

Once out of the church, Sebastian assures Father Vita that he has regained his composure and that his assistance is no longer needed.

SEBASTIAN

Father, I'm much better now. I just needed a little fresh air. I don't know what got into me.

They reach the rectory and Sebastian wishes to be alone.

SEBASTIAN

I'm just going inside and lying down...rest myself for a while.

FATHER VITA

Are you sure, my son? I'd be glad to pray with you in hopes of lifting this heavy burden from your heart.

SEBASTIAN

No thanks, Father. I'll be all right. Only God can help me now.

As Sebastian hurries into the rectory, Father Vita stares at him while holding his rosary beads and crucifix. Then he recites "In the name of the Father, the Son, and the Holy Spirit" and kisses it.

SCENE 4: MORNING OF THE FIELD TRIP

Dr. Lovette is the first to arrive at the university standing out front at the van awaiting the arrival of her students. They gradually start to appear, the first one being Justine, who prides herself on being on time.

JUSTINE COATES

Good morning, Doctor. I had my clock set for 5:00 a.m., although I knew we weren't leaving until 9:00 a.m. It's important to me to be on time if not early to any and all events.

Dr. Lovette smiles.

DR. LOVETTE

Very good.

Then Samantha arrives, hitching a ride from Kyle, of course, who was more than glad to oblige. And immediately behind them was Damian, who was verbally

37

attacked by the others as he exited his very expensive sports car.

JUSTINE COATES

So you decided to join the peasants, huh?

Damian condescendingly responds.

DAMIAN LOVECRAFT

Well, I had nothing else to do, and since I seldom attend my own church, I thought I'd just as well tag along to this one.

JUSTINE COATES

How kind of you.

Next, Warren arrives, a cab drops him off.

Damian sarcastically comments.

DAMIAN LOVECRAFT

Catching a cab, what a shame. I wonder if he had enough for a tip.

No one finds his joke amusing. And, last but not least, Josh arrives pedaling his bike.

DR. LOVETTE

Good, everyone's here. Get ready to load up. Make sure you only have the things you need, which we discussed, and remember the rules we went over...We're on a quest, so have respect. OK, let's hit the road.

Everyone loads into the van and they drive off en route to The Church of All Saints.

SCENE 5: FINAL SERVICE AT THE CHURCH OF ALL SAINTS

It is a bright and sunny Sunday morning in May, the last Sunday The Church of All Saints will be opening its doors to its parishioners. Following Mass, Bishop Quintus will be performing the deconsecration ceremony. It's a relatively small crowd, as many of the parishioners, both saddened and disappointed over the closing, have opted not to attend what obviously is the end of a very important part of their lives.

Father Vita appeals to the parishioners not to have a heavy heart, but to try and find a way to endure this horrendous sacrifice.

FATHER VITA

Just remember, this building where we stand is only a shell. The spirit of God lives within our hearts.

He looks to the Holy Tabernacle placed near the altar, the same one that had been placed there over two hundred –twenty five years ago. Father Vita takes this opportunity to tell the story—one he has told on many occasions—of those who came before, who built The Church of All Saints, and the history of the bronze Holy Tabernacle they brought with them to this new world.

FATHER VITA

The year was 1780, when a group of Roman Catholics from Italy, lead by the great Father Demetric, traveled to this new land. They were the first Roman Catholics to colonize here after the Dutch and French. History will tell you that it was much later, a fact that has been challenged over the years...but we know the truth, and that's what matters. It took everything they had of value to make the journey, but once here they labored tirelessly to build this great church, the first Roman Catholic Church built in this area, though not recognized by many as being so. They built this church with their bare hands, stone by stone. And upon its completion in 1789, they placed the Holy Tabernacle here, a gift bestowed them by the archbishop from their region in Rome, which is said to have been blessed by a saint. This Holy Tabernacle has never been disturbed or removed...that is until today. This is indeed an unforgettable day for the community of The Church

> *of All Saints. We welcome Bishop Quintus to perform the deconsecration. So now without further ado, Bishop Quintus will perform the deconsecration ceremony.*

As Bishop Quintus begins, what started as a bright and sunny day now gives off a gray overcast, blanketing the church, shadowing the beautiful stained glass windows. It is very noticeable to those inside but the bishop continues with the ceremony.

Father Vita, standing at a distance, gestures to the two altar servers to prepare to lift the Holy Tabernacle, at which time Bishop Quintus proceeds with the deconsecration ceremony. At the conclusion, the bishop makes it official with two final words.

BISHOP

> *I hereby relegate this church…The Church of All Saints…to "profane use."*

As these two words spill from the bishop's mouth, there is an air of solemnity and a sigh of despair and grief from the audience. As this is unfolding, the church begins to shake. It feels like a tremor is moving the church almost violently. It is strong enough that cracks and seams run down the walls. It feels as though the entire church is settling, for the first time in its existence. The parishioners as well as Father Vita are alarmed by these events. Some are even frightened, but they remain and quietly pray. As abruptly as it starts, it just stops.

Father Vita offers words of comfort.

FATHER VITA

Please do not be alarmed. This is a very solid building, though past her prime, one that has served its time gracefully.

Father Vita provides the altar servers with final instructions.

FATHER VITA

Please remove the Holy Tabernacle from the column.

As the two altar servers remove the Holy Tabernacle housing the Blessed Sacrament/Eucharist, a horrible stink engulfs the building. A smell so offensive some of the parishioners cough and gag. A child even regurgitates.

As this is unfolding, Sebastian is in the basement on bended knee, clenching his crucifix, praying with all his might. Below in the sub-basement, the columbarium wall is disrupted due to the shaking, causing some of the faceplates and urns to fall to the floor. Back in the church, the parishioners, overtaken by the foul odor, hurry out, practically running each other over.

FATHER VITA

Careful, careful, everyone, please take your time.

Father Vita, barely able to withstand the smell himself, gestures to the servers to exit the building and to bring the Holy Tabernacle with them.

FATHER VITA

Take it to the rectory for now. Once we vacate the premises, we will have to find another home for it. Perhaps we will donate it to another church.

SCENE 6: OUTSIDE THE CHURCH OF ALL SAINTS

As Father Vita hastily exits the church, Dr. Lovette and her students drive up in their van. As they are getting out of the van, Father Vita approaches them and introduces himself.

FATHER VITA

Hello, I'm Father Vita, may I help you?

DR. LOVETTE

Hello, Father. I'm Dr. Lovette, from the university, and these are my students.

FATHER VITA

Oh, yes, we've been expecting you. Welcome to The Church of All Saints. Although this is a sad day for the community of Sleepwater and its parishioners, we are happy to open the doors to The Church of All Saints to give those with a passion for great architecture a last opportunity to observe her beauty.

DR. LOVETTE

Thank you, Father. We truly appreciate your kindness and that of the diocese for allowing us this opportunity.

The students are anxious and ready to go exploring.

DR. LOVETTE

OK, you guys, let's do a little sightseeing out here. Then we'll move inside. Don't get lost.

Everyone disburses in different directions. While still standing together, a tall and very handsome man approaches Father Vita and Dr. Lovette.

FATHER VITA

Oh, you made it. Let me introduce the two of you. Dr. Lovette, this is Jeff Midtomac, the photojournalist I mentioned to you over the phone, who would be here as well as you and your students. He is here to take final photos of this magnificent structure, and Dr. Lovette and her students are here to explore and take in the wonder of this structure before it's demolished.

48

DR. LOVETTE

You photograph historic churches?

JEFF MIDTOMAC

Yes, when I'm not capturing heartache and despair.

DR. LOVETTE

Yes, I would say...I'm somewhat familiar with your work. Your coverage of the war in Uganda was pretty intense.

Father Vita interrupts.

FATHER VITA

Well, there are many things to be done before The Church of All Saints closes its doors forever. I will leave the two of you to become acquainted. By the way, be very careful during your expedition. We were experiencing mild structural shaking earlier as Bishop Quintus was performing our deconsecration ritual. Can't imagine what happened, old church settling perhaps. Just be careful and stay together as much as possible...for your safety, you understand.

Dr. Lovette turns her attention to Jeff.

DR. LOVETTE

Well I must ask...What brings a renowned photojournalist such as you to a soon-to-be demolished Roman Catholic church? The stories you've covered and uncovered, and the danger and intrigue...well, let's just say you have quite an impressive reputation as a photojournalist.

JEFF MIDTOMAC

Wow, I'm impressed.

DR. LOVETTE

Well, when Father Vita mentioned that a re-nowned photojournalist would be here today and he gave me your name...I just took the liberty of going on the computer and doing a little investigating, and, well, I too was impressed.

He smiles but does not offer an explanation.

JEFF MIDTOMAC

Thank you.

DR. LOVETTE

I'm sorry. I don't mean to pry.

JEFF MIDTOMAC

No, it's all right.

He hesitates.

JEFF MIDTOMAC

I guess you could say I've been on a sabbatical of sorts, but when I heard yet another Roman Catholic church was closing, I felt a need to do a piece on it.

His tone changes; it appears humble.

JEFF MIDTOMAC

Sometimes you need to balance yourself, not only in your personal life but also your career.

His tone picks up.

JEFF MIDTOMAC

Having reported on so many high-profile events and topics, I've decided to take a different road. Not to say I've given up on the high adrenaline rush of hardcore journalism, but with the closing and demolition of this church, among other denominations across the country, I decided to take a closer look here at home, do some pro bono work in this country in hopes of sustaining what's important such as these historical monuments.

He smiles.

JEFF MIDTOMAC

Now I'm preaching. OK, Doctor, now let's talk about you.

She looks surprised.

JEFF MIDTOMAC

Yes, you, Dr. Leslie Lovette. You're no stranger yourself to the media, with your reputation as a prolific architect and of course the rallies and protests you've made in the news with your fight for historic preservations in this country. Not to mention awards for design preservation, and preservations for buildings such as this one. And we must not forget the numerous offers made to you by some of the most prestigious firms on the East Coast, all of which you turned down...if I'm correct.

She smiles.

JEFF MIDTOMAC

I also understand there was an offer for a Director of Architecture position offered at your university, which you also turned down, to which Dr. Alexandria Haigler was appointed later.

She's amazed.

DR. LOVETTE

Wow, you've done your homework also. I'm impressed.

JEFF MIDTOMAC

Well, the first thing I did when I decided to go in this direction was to find out who was out there in the area of preservation for what many consider historical churches, and your name kept popping up. So when I contacted Father Vita and he mentioned Dr. Lovette, architect, and a group of students would be exploring the place before demolition, well, let's just say, the timing seemed perfect.

Dr. Lovette blushes and appears bashful; he notices.

JEFF MIDTOMAC

Well, I'm going to get my gear and take a few exterior shots. Will you and your students be around for a while?

DR. LOVETTE

Sure, we just got here. Take a look around. As you can see, they're in total amazement.

JEFF MIDTOMAC

OK, so I'm sure we'll run into each other before we leave.

DR. LOVETTE

Sounds good. Perhaps we'll collaborate on some of the findings and architectural details we come across. A pair of eyes coming from different perspectives could be a good thing for all of us.

JEFF MIDTOMAC

Yes, that does sound good.

As Dr. Lovette and Jeff go their separate ways and Dr. Lovette turns to walk away, she and the groundskeeper,

Sebastian, bump into each other. He appears nervous, frantic, disheveled, and in a rush.

DR. LOVETTE

Oh, I'm sorry, sir, I—

He cuts her off hastily.

SEBASTIAN

You must leave here!

Dr. Lovette is confused.

DR. LOVETTE

Excuse me?

SEBASTIAN

You must leave here, take your group with you, and never return here.

DR. LOVETTE

I don't understand.

SEBASTIAN

You must leave this place and never come back.

DR. LOVETTE

I assure you, we weren't trespassing. We have the diocese's permission to be here.

SEBASTIAN

You don't understand, this place is no longer safe. You're all in danger.

Sebastian notices Father Vita approaching, so he hurries away. Dr. Lovette, out of curiosity, questions Father Vita.

DR. LOVETTE

That man, he was quite adamant that my students and I should not be here. I tried to explain to him that we have permission to be on the premises, but I don't think he believed me.

FATHER VITA

Oh, don't mind him. He's Sebastian, our groundskeeper/handyman. He's lived in these parts his entire life, most recently right here on the church premises in the rectory. Comes from strong superstitious beliefs. Don't worry, he's harmless; he hasn't been himself since the announcing of the church's closing. It hit Sebastian pretty hard, but not only him.

Many of our parishioners are saddened by the event. Anyway, now that the deconsecration of the church is complete, The Church of All Saints is considered "for profane use." You and your students may enter.

DR. LOVETTE

Thank you, Father Vita. I assure you, we will take great care in maintaining the integrity of the church. The students have been instructed on the importance of entering this structure with the same respect granted a holy institution and to remember we are here as guests.

FATHER VITA

Very well, I will not be available for the remainder of the day. I will be journeying to a neighboring church two counties over. No one will be here until tomorrow morning when the new owners arrive, but Sebastian will be here if you need anything. He lives here on the premises and can usually be found in the rectory quarters. He has nowhere else to live, and he has been a great help to the church, as his father before him and his before him. As I said before, the closing of the church has had a profound effect on him, and with no place to go...well, his destiny is in God's hands now.

Dr. Lovette extends her hand to Father Vita.

DR. LOVETTE

Thank you, Father. You've been a great help.

As she turns to walk away and rejoin her students, she notices Sebastian standing in the rectory doorway watching her from a distance. Once he's aware that she notices him watching her, he steps back into the rectory and closes the door. He immediately drops to his knees, and while clenching his rosary, begins to pray to God in a Latin tongue with everything he has, for protection for not only himself but for all of the residents of Sleepwater, including its visitors.

Dr. Lovette goes to gather her students.

DR. LOVETTE

OK, everyone, let's get started. I hope no one forgot anything. Make sure you have your cameras, recorders, journals, whatever you're going to use to document this event. Is everyone ready?

They all nod that they're ready to go.

SCENE 7: TOUR OF THE CHURCH'S EXTERIOR

Dr. Lovette, enthused, expresses her passion for the décor.

DR. LOVETTE

I absolutely adore historical churches, particularly Roman Catholic, because of the history and artistic adornments, particularly this one, which follows the work of Charles Borromeo's Instructiones. This type of architecture was a prominent guide for Roman architecture. OK, the first place and best place to start when examining a historic structure such as a church is the main entrance. As you can see, as was displayed on the projector, it's a classic "Borromeo" inspirational exterior, with the three-pointed doorway façade with the central door being the largest of the three. Borromeo felt that a church's exterior, especially the entryway, needed to set the stage, and be prominent and extraordinary. Also, you can see that the large square-projecting tower at the top of the church dominates the façade. This type of façade was created during the eighteenth and early nineteenth century, as stated in class. Let's move to the inside.

SCENE 8: TOUR OF THE CHURCH'S INTERIOR

Dr. Lovette continues with the tour.

DR. LOVETTE

Now, inside you get a look at an example of the Gothic elements, which were inspired by the Santa Maria Sopra Minerva. Its Gothic inspiration can be seen in the piers and rib vaults, which have been dated back to the thirteenth century. Combined with Borromeo's architectural principles dictated in his Instructiones, this masterpiece was created.

The students are in awe from an architectural viewpoint. It is an honor for them to be the last to walk down the aisle and the last to walk out of the doors.

Jeff enters the church snapping photos. Dr. Lovette walks over to him.

DR. LOVETTE

Amazing, isn't it?

He continues snapping photos and then turns his attention to her.

JEFF MIDTOMAC

Very much so. You know I've seen a lot through this lens, most of which was sorrow and pain...but this...let's just say is a welcome sight...just an unfortunate occasion. Though I must admit, with your reputation for the preservation of structures such as this one, I'm surprised you're not here putting up a fight. Instead you seem to have just accepted it.

DR. LOVETTE

Oh, believe me, I fought, but once all the negotiations had been settled and the signatures were on the dotted lines, I just decided to take the loss and turn it into a win for my students. Being able to get them in here before it completely disappears seems to be the only victory with this fight. I want this experience to be one that will inspire them and expand their imaginations. To become great contributors to the field of architecture, to get firsthand experience of a time gone by, and to never forget the work of the masters, regardless of what the future holds.

JEFF MIDTOMAC

Good idea.

Following her heartfelt speech, she notices him fumbling around with his camera.

DR. LOVETTE

Tell me, what do you really see when you look through that lens?

He smiles as he continues taking snapshots.

JEFF MIDTOMAC

Well, sometimes that's a tough one...I guess you would say "a story."

DR. LOVETTE

Would that be every time you look through it?

He pauses and smiles.

JEFF MIDTOMAC

Yes, pretty much so.

DR. LOVETTE

Well, what do you see here?

He looks through his lens.

JEFF MIDTOMAC

Well, the obvious…history, beauty, and something I'm not quite able to put my finger on.

DR. LOVETTE

Yes, old structures such as this one do seem to evoke an air of mystery.

He looks a little unsettled.

DR. LOVETTE

Are you OK?

He hesitates for a moment.

JEFF MIDTOMAC

Yes, I'm fine.

One of the students calls Dr. Lovette down to the altar.

DR. LOVETTE

Excuse me.

JEFF MIDTOMAC

Sure.

Jeff continues taking snapshots, when from the entry-way Sebastian appears through his lens, startling him.

JEFF MIDTOMAC

Hello, can we help you?

Dr. Lovette walks back to Jeff.

DR. LOVETTE

He's Sebastian, the groundskeeper/handyman. He lives here on the premises.

Dr. Lovette moves toward Sebastian.

DR. LOVETTE

Please come in. Perhaps you can give us a tour, tell us about any undocumented events you may have heard of…since you've been here for so many years…according to Father Vita, that is.

Sebastian just stands there, inches away from the threshold leading into the church.

Samantha whispers to Josh.

SAMANTHA PRENTISS

Creepy!

Josh snickers.

Sebastian still stands behind the threshold, careful not to cross it.

SEBASTIAN

Why are you still here? I warned you it's not safe to be here.

Damian condescendingly interjects.

DAMIAN LOVECRAFT

Is that a threat...handyman?

DR. LOVETTE

Please, Damian.

She turns her attention back to Sebastian and tries to reassure him that there's not a problem.

DR. LOVETTE

Yes, I remember your warning, but believe me the structure of this building is sound. We just have to make sure we're not here when the demolition team arrives.

He does not appreciate her humor and simply stands there in silence.

DR. LOVETTE

Father Vita granted us full permission to be here. When he left he even suggested we contact you if we needed anything. He said you'd be able to help since you've lived in the area your entire life.

SEBASTIAN

You've been warned.

He turns and proceeds to walk away when Jeff stops him.

JEFF MIDTOMAC

What do you mean by that? If you have something to say, just say it.

Sebastian stops and turns around and addresses Jeff.

SEBASTIAN

Many, many years ago, my great-great-great-grandfather was handed a responsibility, which he passed on to his son, and he to his son, until it reached me. The responsibility was to oversee and protect the sanctity of this church, but as a result of today's actions, I can never again cross this threshold, for it is no longer blessed and no longer sacred. I now fear for this community and what's to come. So do yourselves a favor and leave this place before it's too late, though it might already be.

The groundskeeper's remarks arouse Jeff's curiosity.

JEFF MIDTOMAC

Sebastian, is it? I can understand your being upset because of the church closing, but is there something else you're trying to say…with the warning and all?

SEBASTIAN

There is nothing else to say; you've been warned.

He turns and walks back to the rectory.

Jeff reaches out and is about to call him, but Dr. Lovette interjects.

DR. LOVETTE

Perhaps we should let him go on about his business. We wouldn't want to antagonize him any more than he already is.

SAMANTHA PRENTISS

Like I said...creepy.

KYLE QUENTIN

This guy talks like the closing of this church is the end of the world.

Kyle then puts on his facial and vocal rendition of *Dracula*.

KYLE QUENTIN

Before this night is over, the end of the world will come as a blessing.

No one finds it amusing except Kyle himself and Samantha.

JUSTINE COATES

It's obvious he comes from strong religious beliefs. Dr. Lovette, you did say he's lived here for years. He's probably been very isolated, so any myths and legends passed down to him through the generations are probably pretty much all he knows. No wonder he's frightful of what's next for him now that the church is closing.

Samantha and Damian stand together cackling at Justine's synopsis of Sebastian, while Jeff sinks into thought.

JEFF MIDTOMAC

OK, if you say so.

Dr. Lovette notices Jeff's demeanor, but she's called away by one of the students. Jeff continues in thought with a look of concern, perhaps unsettled by Sebastian's mysterious predictions.

Down near the altar, Dr. Lovette conveys to the students that it's time to get back on the road.

DR. LOVETTE

It's getting late, and it gets really dark up here. The back roads we have to take to the city are pretty dark at night...no streetlights, unlike in the city, just darkness and curvy roads. Besides, there was a severe storm forecast on the news this morning before we left for later today. So grab your belongings. We're heading out.

Josh Morrow, self-proclaimed adventurer, chimes in.

JOSH MORROW

Come on, Doc, this can't be all there is to see.

DR. LOVETTE

Yes, it is for us.

DAMIAN LOVECRAFT

I can't believe I'm saying this...but Morrow may be on to something. Come on, Doc, you can't honestly say that you're not interested in...how should I say it...getting down to the bare bones of this old place.

The rest of the crew cheers him on.

DR. LOVETTE

No, no, no, the diocese was nice enough to let us come in here and take a look around before the new owners take over. They made it clear that we were welcome to explore the grounds and the church's exterior as well as the interior, and we promised to be respectful and not disturb or disrupt anything.

KYLE QUENTIN

That's cool, Doc, but we all know that an old church like this one has to have more to it than what we've seen so far.

The other students chime in, supporting Kyle's observation.

JEFF MIDTOMAC

Seems you're outnumbered, Doctor.

DR. LOVETTE

Yes, it's starting to look that way. Well, they did say the interior as well as the exterior. And Father Vita did not specify any areas we were forbidden to roam. He just said to be careful because there had been some mild structural shaking earlier, but he didn't seem alarmed.

There's silence from the students, eagerly awaiting her acceptance of the plan.

DR. LOVETTE

OK, if we're going to look deeper, we're going to do it my way and by my rules...got it?

They all respond harmoniously in agreement.

DR. LOVETTE

OK, it just so happens that I bought a copy of the church's blueprints with me.

The students are enthused, all except Warren, who appears to be low-key. They knew it would be impossible for her not to explore the entire skeletal structure of this absolutely magnificent edifice.

Dr. Lovette spreads the blueprints out on the altar and reads it out loud.

DR. LOVETTE

As you can see here on the blueprint, this entire interior area is made up of the pews, the altar, and a few other rooms here on the same floor. It's a good-sized space, and the façade makes it look even larger.

She continues reading.

DR. LOVETTE

Um, this is strange.

Everyone has a look of curiosity, awaiting an explanation.

WARREN SYKES

Is anything wrong, Doctor?

She responds in an intriguing tone.

DR. LOVETTE

Well sort of...kind of.

She pauses, then continues.

DR. LOVETTE

According to this blueprint, there is a significant amount of dead space here just beyond this wall along the east side of the basement. There are no other rooms specified on these blueprints.

WARREN SYKES

There just appears to be a solid wall there.

DR. LOVETTE

Yes, but as you can see from an architectural standpoint, it just doesn't make sense to have such an abundance of dead space in an area not being used as a functional space.

WARREN SYKES

Yes, I see what you mean.

JOSH MORROW

Now that's what I'm talking about. I knew there was more to this place than meets the eye.

The others support Josh's enthusiasm.

DR. LOVETTE

Hold on, everyone, let's calm down.

She continues studying the blueprint.

DR. LOVETTE

Well, according to this, there is definitely something behind that wall that leads to another location.

JEFF MIDTOMAC

Do you think this is a good idea?

DR. LOVETTE

I'm sorry. I didn't even ask you your opinion. I know you're not with our little group, but it was insensitive of me to not ask your opinion before we decided to embark on this adventure.

He smiles slightly and then responds.

JEFF

No offense taken. As a journalist, I understand your insatiable need to find out what's on the other side.

He pauses for a moment.

JEFF MIDTOMAC

So yes…I'm in.

DR. LOVETTE

Great! We might just make history here today. OK, since there is obviously no hole in the wall, there is probably another way to get in there…we just have to find it.

SCENE 9: JOURNEY TO THE BASEMENT

Everyone gathers their belongings and makes their way down a hallway that leads to the basement stairway, when from the windows they notice Sebastian. He's standing motionless, with his crucifix clenched in his hands. He is praying with all his might, but they are unable to hear, due to the thickness of the window panes and the distance he's standing from the church. They watch him for a moment but proceed in their quest. Eventually they reach the basement.

JUSTIN COATES

It's huge down here.

DR. LOVETTE

Yes, it's the equivalent of two large city blocks, the same as the main floor.

JOSH MORROW

There's nothing but junk down here.

JUSTIN COATES

Keep an open mind, Morrow.

The group begins to explore the basement, hoping to unfold secrets and mysteries of the past. After a pretty good look around, Dr. Lovett comes to the same conclusion as Josh.

DR. LOVETTE

Well, guys, everything down here looks pretty ordinary. A few old broken-down pews, some very old hymnal books, out-of-commission organs, and lots of dust. Hey, someone's been hanging out down here; there are footprints everywhere.

DAMIAN LOVECRAFT

I'd put money on it. This is "Psycho Sebastian's" pad. Handyman by day, madman by night.

No one finds him amusing, except Samantha.

Kyle Quentin, in his prankster mood, hits some of the keys on one of the organs.

KYLE QUENTIN

Well, this one sure needs to be tuned.

Everyone ignores him.

Dr. Lovette looks at her watch.

DR. LOVETTE

It's getting late. It will be getting dark soon, and a storm is in the forecast. We had better start back to the city.

Dr. Lovette turns her attention to Jeff, who's taking shots of the soon-to-be demolished basement.

DR. LOVETTE

Well, we're heading back to the city. What direction are you traveling in?

JEFF MIDTOMAC

Actually, I'm heading into the city also. I have to send my images to my picture editor, who will review them. Once the images are viewed, and depending on the size of the article I'm going to write, images will be selected for the article. Then I will write what is referred to as a "picture article."

DR. LOVETTE

Sounds interesting. I look forward to reading it. Anyway, it's been nice meeting you, and good luck with the article.

JEFF MIDTOMAC

Thanks.

As the group is walking toward the door, Damian stumbles and trips on a book. Of course this annoys him.

DAMIAN LOVECRAFT

What the...!

Justine hurries over and picks the book up. She is overwhelmed by its apparent intrigue and possible history.

JUSTINE COATES

Hey, Dr. Lovette, take a look at this.

Dr. Lovette joins Justine along with her classmates... except for Damian, who does not appear interested in anything resembling a relic.

JUSTINE COATES

Isn't it intriguing, Doctor?

Dr. Lovette inspects the exterior of the book.

DR. LOVETTE

Yes…very.

JUSTINE COATES

How old would you say it is? A hundred, perhaps a hundred and fifty years old?

Dr. Lovette appears consumed with the book as she continues examining its exterior.

DR. LOVETTE

No…I would say more like two hundred years, perhaps older.

Samantha, who at first had only a passing interest, now appears enthused.

SAMANTHA PRENTISS

Wow, a two hundred-year-old book. Pass it on; I want to see what's inside.

DR. LOVETTE

Hold on, everyone. This book is very fragile and perhaps valuable and/or sacred. We need to be very careful when handling it. Take a look here at the binding, even the texture of the cover. This book most likely predates the nineteenth century.

JOSH MORROW

I knew this old place was filled with secrets.

DR. LOVETTE

Well, it will have to be turned over to the diocese, or worse, the new owners.

KYLE QUENTIN

Hey, whatever happened to finders keepers?

DAMIAN LOVECRAFT

For once, I have to agree with Quentin.

As Damian walks away he murmurs.

DAMIAN LOVECRAFT

Now that's scary.

Warren Sykes moves forward out of his shell.

WARREN SYKES

Dr. Lovette, the inscription says "Souls of the Damned." It would be interesting to see what's in it.

Damian makes a sarcastic remark about Warren to Samantha.

DAMIAN LOVECRAFT

I guess the "good student" does speak.

SAMANTHA PRENTISS

Oh, you're just jealous because he's tall, handsome, and doesn't feed into your egotistical mentality.

DAMIAN LOVECRAFT

Prentiss, as usual, you've come up with the wrong answer. No wonder you have to "slut" up to losers just to pass your classes.

Samantha is amused at Damian's obvious insecurities, which clearly indicate that she's correct in her assumption of him.

Dr. Lovette and Warren are still examining the book's exterior.

DR. LOVETTE

It is both my professional opinion and gut instinct that tells me this book holds mysteries and secrets of the past.

WARREN SYKES

What do you think, Doctor?

Dr. Lovette stares at the book for a moment.

DR. LOVETTE

Let's do it!

As she is about to open the book, the church experiences another tremor but stronger than the previous one. This time everyone is bounced and thrown about, but no one gets hurt.

DR. LOVETTE

Is everyone OK?

Everyone gathers their composure and collects their belongings once the tremors stop.

DR. LOVETTE

Father Vita mentioned that something like this happened earlier. We'd better get out of here.

As they are about to leave, Warren notices an area in the wall that looks suspicious. The area was bulging, as if weakened. It was the width of a door frame. So they gather to inspect it. They soon realize it's a fake wall, and the seam covering it was probably disturbed as a result of the shifting, revealing a concealed passageway.

DR. LOVETTE

What in the world...? I guess this explains that dead space on the blueprints, but more importantly, where does it lead?

Jeff rubs the wall, following an apparent seam, probing what turns out to be an entrance that has been plastered.

JEFF MIDTOMAC

This ridge seems to lead to a plastered area, a doorway perhaps.

This is right up Josh's alley.

JOSH MORROW

Now this is what I'm talking about, a secret room.

DR. LOVETTE

We'd better be leaving now. Another tremor like that last one and someone may get hurt.

JEFF MIDTOMAC

I agree. We don't know what's causing these tremors, so let's err on the side of caution and get out of here.

DAMIAN LOVECRAFT

I don't know who invited you on this excursion, but you're not a part of this group.

DR. LOVETTE

OK, Damian, we're all here for the same reason, to experience this part of history before it's gone forever. We've done that, so it's time to leave now.

As the group is about to leave the basement, they experience another tremor, but this one causes major damage. The team is thrown about, and much of the structure comes down, including concrete and debris, particularly around the entrance area. As abruptly as it begins, it stops, leaving that awful stench in the air that had permeated the church earlier. Everyone notices it. Once the tremors subside, everyone starts coming around, slowly, and with difficulty because of the dust and debris. Everyone had taken shelter to avoid injury, but Kyle Quentin, the class comic, is hurt. He lies on the floor, moaning, gripping his right leg. Apparently it's injured. Dr. Lovette rushes over to him to assess his injuries.

DR. LOVETTE

Kyle, let me take a look.

Dr. Lovette applies mild pressure to his upper thigh, where Kyle is holding his leg. He groans as a result of the pain. But he does not want to appear weak, so he tries to cover up the pain by using humor.

KYLE QUENTIN

I'm OK, Doc. See? No more tears.

DR. LOVETTE

Are you sure? When I touched your leg, it looked as if you were in a lot of pain.

Kyle is determined to not look like a wuss.

KYLE QUENTIN

No, I'm just fine.

He tries to get up on his own but is unable to do so, so he elicits help.

KYLE QUENTIN

I could use a hand, just until I get up on my feet.

Dr. Lovette and Warren Sykes help him stand. When he's on his feet and starts to walk, he's a little off balance. It gets better, but he does have a limp.

DR. LOVETTE

Are you all right?

KYLE QUENTIN

Yes, a little sore, but I'm OK. You can't keep a superhero down.

Dr. Lovette looks around.

DR. LOVETTE

Is everyone else OK?

Everyone is now on his or her feet, coughing, dusting off, and looking around. A few bumps and scratches but no major injuries. Dr. Lovette notices Jeff over near the exit assessing the fallout of the tremor. She joins him.

JEFF MIDTOMAC

This is not good.

DR. LOVETTE

We're trapped in here?

JEFF MIDTOMAC

Yes, it looks that way.

Everyone appears frightened, but Damian is frantic at the thought of being trapped. He pushes his way between Dr. Lovette and Jeff to reach the entryway in a feeble attempt to remove the pounds of rubble obstructing the entryway. He panics and starts grabbing and pulling at the rubble blocking the entrance.

DAMIAN LOVECRAFT

Get out of my way! I'm getting the hell out of here.

Dr. Lovette calms him.

DR. LOVETTE

Come on, Damian, pull it together. You're not down here alone…breathe.

Damian takes Dr. Lovette's advice and takes deep, relaxing breaths, calming him down. Damian is not the only one concerned about their predicament. They all are, except for Josh. He's been waiting for a situation just like this.

Everyone starts checking his or her mobile devices, cell phones, iPads, and iPods, but there's no reception.

WARREN SYKES

I can't reach anyone. There doesn't appear to be any reception.

DR. LOVETTE

That doesn't make any sense; we're just in the basement.

SAMANTHA PRENTISS

I hate to side with Lovecraft, but if we can't get out of here, we're going to die.

JOSH MORROW

You know, she could be right. I told my girl I was going to an old church upstate, but I didn't tell her which old church.

JUSTINE COATES

I live alone, so no one will be looking for me.

DR. LOVETTE

Calm down, everyone. The university knows we're here. When I don't show up for class and they're unable to reach me, they'll know to come here. They'll send someone for us.

Dr. Lovette turns her attention back to Jeff.

JEFF MIDTOMAC

Well, from what I can see, we're not getting out of here…not this way, anyway.

WARREN SYKES

There has to be another way out of here.

Damian is jealous of Warren's apparent self-control and straight head.

DAMIEN LOVECRAFT

And Superman speaks!

Warren ignores him, which agitates Damian even more, though he does not show it.

DR. LOVETTE

OK, it looks as if we've been left to our own devices to find a way out of here.

JEFF MIDTOMAC

I say let's start with that suspicious seam in the wall over there.

Jeff leads and everyone else follows. He places his fingers in the seams, and the plaster just starts coming down in pieces. Some of the others join in. Finally enough of the plaster is down to reveal a door with a lock on it. It looks like a lock that could date back a couple of centuries. Warren pays close attention to the lock.

WARREN SYKES

This lock looks like a relic. Probably dates back around the time the church was built… just like the book.

JEFF MIDTOMAC

Take a look around, everyone. See if you can find something hard and heavy that could break this lock. It shouldn't be too hard to break since it looks like it's ready to come off.

Josh hands Jeff a pipe he finds in a corner. Jeff bangs on the lock a couple of times, and it falls off. He opens the door slowly, and everyone who's able to see beyond the door are in amazement. The others start shoving until they're able to see what the others are looking at. Josh is in hysterics with excitement.

SAMANTHA PRENTISS

I wonder how long it's been down there.

Damian condescendingly states the obvious in response to Samantha's question.

DAMIAN LOVECRAFT

Well, off the top of my head, since it's below the basement...I'd say during the time the church was built.

DR. LOVETTE

What in the world...? This wasn't on the blueprints.

The door appears to be the pathway to an undocumented location beneath the church's basement. There are stone and mud walls and a spiral staircase that leads down into what appears to be a sublevel, obviously built when the church was built, though it's not a part of the blueprints. The stone is old, and there are signs of decay, probably as a result of water seeping in over the years, as the structure is apparently underground.

JOSH MORROW

Getting trapped down here is starting to look like a good move. I can't wait to get down there and see what history has left.

JEFF MIDTOMAC

I should probably lead the way. I've been in some pretty hazardous situations in my time.

Damian mumbles.

DAMIAN LOVECRAFT

Like I said before, who put him in charge?

His comment is ignored, since everyone except for Josh is willing to follow anyone with a possible way out.

JEFF MIDTOMAC

Stay alert, everyone. We could be in for more surprises.

As Jeff prepares to lead the group, with Dr. Lovette right behind him, she tries to make light of the situation.

DR. LOVETTE

It's nice of you to take the lead, but you really don't have to. You agreed to come along as our guest, not our guide.

JEFF MIDTOMAC

It's OK, I've been in a few unpredictable situations not so different than this one. Besides, I'm the one with the night vision glasses and flashlight.

He pulls them from out of his duffle bag. Dr. Lovette is impressed.

SCENE 10: JOURNEY TO THE SUBLEVEL

As Jeff moves toward the steps, he makes a cautionary suggestion.

JEFF MIDTOMAC

Hold on!

DR. LOVETTE

What is it?

JEFF MIDTOMAC

We're a few feet away from what appears to be extremely old and probably risky stairs that lead down to another level of the church...a sublevel probably. Obviously something else not listed on the blueprints.

Josh becomes enthused again. Jumping up and down, blurting out the word "yes" repeatedly.

JOSH MORROW

Yes, yes, yes. I knew it!

Dr. Lovette contains Josh's enthusiasm while verbally guiding the team as a whole.

DR. LOVETTE

Hold on, everyone. We don't know the structural integrity of these stairs or the area down below. But what we do know is that this church is very old, so let's think like researchers or explorers and approach this unfamiliar territory with caution. Remember, we went over this in class, so let's put that knowledge to work now.

Everyone is in agreement, so they pull themselves together and prepare to follow Dr. Lovette's command.

JEFF MIDTOMAC

OK, is everyone ready?

There's an echo from the group acknowledging that they're ready to begin this journey. Jeff proceeds in heading the group down the stairs leading to what appears to indeed be a sublevel. Several in the group are coughing and sneezing, the effects of the mold and mildew, making it difficult to breathe, the result of water seeping in, since the room was built underground. It's the perfect location for mold growth.

JOSH MORROW

Man, it smells bad down here.

DR. LOVETTE

Adventure comes with consequences; never forget that.

As he reaches the bottom of the stairs, he notice that the walls and flooring are damp and moist, and that the foundation is basically soil and stone. Jeff finally makes it to bottom.

JEFF MIDTOMAC

Hey guys, come on down. It's not as dark down here as up there.

The rest of the team makes it to the bottom of the stairs.

DR. LOVETTE

Look, be careful. Just observe, don't touch anything, and stay close together. Remember, we're not down here to sightsee. We're just looking for a way out.

Samantha has a gleam in her eyes.

SAMANTHA PRENTISS

Wow, this place sure is spooky. No telling what we may find down here.

DR. LOVETTE

We're not here on a treasure hunt.

Samantha replies under her breath.

SAMANTHA PRENTISS

Speak for yourself.

Josh assures the group.

JOSH MORROW

Trust me. If there's a way out of here, I'll find it.

Kyle limps over to Dr. Lovette.

KYLE QUENTIN

Doctor, this is the most mysterious place I've ever seen. Since we're looking for a way out anyway, can we explore just a little?

The rest of the group chimes in. Dr. Lovette gives in.

DR. LOVETTE

OK, but stay in this general area.

Jeff addresses Dr. Lovette.

JEFF MIDTOMAC

Quite an enthused group you have.

She smiles.

DR. LOVETTE

Yes, they remind me of myself in undergrad and grad school. Being enthused and excited, searching for the next adventure. Their zest and energy to explore and learn is really why I enjoy teaching.

JEFF MIDTOMAC

Well, if we intend to find another way out of here, we'd better do some exploring ourselves.

DR. LOVETTE

You're right.

SAMANTHA PRENTISS

Why would anyone build a secret floor anyway?

At first it appears to just be an unfinished subbasement floor. Justine is around a corner shouting and screaming for Dr. Lovette to come. Her teacher comes running, with the rest of the group following. Once they reach Justine, everyone just stands there staring, mesmerized, and speechless.

Josh is the first one to speak.

JOSH MORROW

Holy...shit.

Dr. Lovette, while still staring, reacts to Josh's comment.

DR. LOVETTE

Watch your language; this is still a church.

Finally everyone appears to be coming out of their trance after looking at a wall with what appears to be hundreds of little boxes affixed to it.

JEFF MIDTOMAC

Well, this might just answer the question, "Why would anyone build a secret floor?"

Dr. Lovette walks closer to the wall, observing the structure, and finally touches it. She appears to be intoxicated by it.

DR. LOVETTE

This is absolutely amazing.

Samantha is totally oblivious as to what it is.

SAMANTHA PRENTISS

This has to be the scariest thing I've ever seen. What is it?

Justine is annoyed by Samantha's ignorance.

JUSTINE COATES

Are you kidding? It's a columbarium wall for heaven's sake.

Samantha rolls her eyes at Justine behind her back.

Justine, with stars in her eyes, expresses excitement by smiling, glowing and jumping around.

JUSTINE COATES

Wow, this sure is a well-kept secret. I wonder how long it's been here; it looks really old.

SAMANTHA PRENTISS

Will someone enlighten me on this obviously important...find?

Samantha is probably the only one not familiar with what a columbarium is, but Dr. Lovette schools everyone.

DR. LOVETTE

Well, as some of you may know, a columbarium is a wall used to place the ashes of the dead. The bodies are cremated, then the ashes of the deceased are placed in vessels known as urns. Then the urns are respectfully inurned within the niches in the walls, as you see here. It's an alternative to earthen burials. Historically, Roman columbaria were known to be built in the underground or lower levels of the church, such as this one. And since this is a Roman Catholic church, it seems logical, although traditional earthen burial is preferred.

KYLE QUENTIN

So how did these lucky stiffs end up down here? There appears to be hundreds of them.

Jeff is walking around taking snapshots.

JEFF MIDTOMAC

During my travels, I've had the opportunity to explore some magnificent and dangerous locations. Ruins, catacombs, caves…you name it, but an undocumented columbarium, beneath a church…well…I think this is a first.

Damian snarls at Jeff's comment under his breath.

DR. LOVETTE

Well, it's my first also.

WARREN SYKES

It looks really old. Any idea how long it's been here?

DR. LOVETTE

This wall wears the face of pain. Smothered in decay, mold, discoloration, and damaged stone, the byproducts of neglect. It's very old, so old that all of the niches have petrified into the earth, encased themselves deep into the walls of the church's foundation, which is mostly dirt. It's probably because the church has settled quite a bit over the past two hundred years.

She struggles to read the inscription on a few of the niches.

DR. LOVETTE

Some of the faceplates are missing.

JUSTINE COATES

They're not missing. Some seem to have fallen off, some even broken. I'll collect what I can find and try to piece them together. We may even be able to figure out which niche goes with which faceplate.

DR. LOVETTE

I'm trying to read the inscription on a few of the faceplates, but the print has thinned, second to aging.

Jeff hands her the flashlight.

JEFF MIDTOMAC

Here, see if this helps.

Dr. Lovette takes the flashlight and moves in closer toward the niches.

DR. LOVETTE

This is amazing, absolutely amazing.

Everyone hurries over to Dr. Lovette to find out the reason for her enthusiasm.

DR. LOVETTE

This is just…I just can't believe it. This has to be the find of the century.

The group is eager for Dr. Lovette to share what she's uncovered.

DR. LOVETTE

It's the dates on some of the niches.

SAMANTHA PRENTISS

What about them?

Dr. Lovette works to gain her composure.

DR. LOVETTE

OK, let me calm myself.

She takes a deep breath and continues to explore the wall, with the flashlight.

DR. LOVETTE

Well, there appears to be hundreds of them, though I shouldn't be surprised. The mortality rate during the seventeenth century was very high. And from what I can see, some of these niches are dated 1810 through 1814, some even 1820, and it goes on. Some of the faceplates are broken off, and the urns have fallen out and broken. Here's a piece...I can make out some of the inscription. Its date is 1829, and part of the name is "Father." I think this is all I'm going to be able to find on this one. Whoever this person was, he was the last to be buried. See, it's right beneath the last niche. There are no numbered niches after this one.

Justine joins Dr. Lovette.

JUSTINE COATES

Here's a piece of a faceplate I found over there on the floor. It's dated 1804, and above is the number one. I can't make out the name. Probably the first to be buried here. I can't find the rest of the faceplate. There are more broken pieces here, but the inscriptions are not easy to figure out.

KYLE QUENTIN

Doctor, you know this could be considered one of those finds of the century.

Samantha is clueless.

SAMANTHA PRENTISS

Yes, why is that?

Now Damian is annoyed by Samantha's lack of knowledge.

DAMIAN LOVECRAFT

Come on, Prentiss, at least try.

SAMANTHA PRENTISS

Like you know what he's alluding to.

DAMIAN LOVECRAFT

I know you don't.

DR. LOVETTE

OK, guys, let's be nice to each other. What I think Kyle is alluding to, which is pretty special, is that these dates predate the first officially documented cremations in this country. Now, according to history, the first recorded cremation in the US was in 1792. However, the first crematorium was built in Pennsylvania, in 1876, and the second, also in Pennsylvania, in 1884. Prior to the 1800s, cremations were rarely recorded; therefore most will declare that the official date for cremations in this country is between 1876 and 1884. Depending on which research source you review, these dates could vary by a year or two.

JUSTINE COATES

This being a burial site, combined with the dates on the faceplates predating 1876, could be enough to declare the church a historical site, or at least slow down the demolition slated to start in the morning.

Jeff is still walking around taking snapshots.

JEFF MIDTOMAC

I was expecting to write a farewell piece, but as it turns out, I might be writing about a "stay of execution."

DR. LOVETTE

I sure hope so.

JOSH MORROW

This place is huge. If this wall has been secretly down here, there's no telling what else we may find.

DAMIAN LOVECRAFT

Speaking for myself, the only thing I'm interested in finding right now is a way out of here.

KYLE QUENTIN

This place is creepy.

DR. LOVETTE

OK, let's get started.

JEFF MIDTOMAC

Look, this place has a pretty big footprint. It has the same dimensions as the entire church.

DAMIAN LOVETTE

So what!

JEFF MIDTOMAC

Well, it stands to reason that since this sub-level is beneath the main floor, as is the basement, the dimensions are the same. And we all know this church is huge. Which means we need to find a way out of here before those dozers start knocking this place down. We need to split up.

JUSTINE COATES

And, Dr. Lovette, if that happens we'll lose all hope of the church being saved…and us to…you know what I mean.

Dr. Lovette turns her attention to Jeff.

DR. LOVETTE

OK. How do you suggest we do this?

DAMIAN LOVETTE

Who's this guy? What makes him an authority? I'm not following him anywhere.

Jeff is starting to lose his patience with Damian and his condescending attitude.

JEFF MIDTOMAC

Da-mon is it?

DAMIAN LOVETTE

No! Damian.

JEFF MIDTOMAC

OK, Damian. Look, I'm not trying to be in charge. It's just that in my line of work, I've been in a few dangerous and unpredictable situations, many similar to this one. I'm just saying that...

Damian starts to laugh, loudly.

DAMIAN LOVECRAFT

You must be kidding me. With so much new digital technology, and "citizen journalism," particularly in the area of photography, with "your line of work," anyone with a cell phone these days...an amateur...could do your job. Aren't you afraid of becoming obsolete? Besides, who needs newspapers or any other paper reading material anymore when we have computers?

Jeff looks shocked and a little embarrassed, as if his secret fear has been revealed. But he's able to make a comeback.

JEFF MIDTOMAC

Well, modern photojournalism has been around since the mid 1920s, when the first 35 mm camera was invented. I'd like to think that since it's survived Argus C, 1939, Asahiflex 11b, 1954, and the invention of the digital camera in the 1990s, it can hold up against this new wave of mobile technology.

Damian looks defeated and simply walks away.

DR. LOVETTE

Damian, that's enough. We're all on edge and really want to get out of here, so please try and control your abuse.

Dr. Lovette turns back to Jeff.

DR. LOVETTE

Jeff, what were you about to say?

Before he's able to respond, the group is overwhelmed by a foul odor that almost takes their breath away.

KYLE QUENTIN

What in the world is that odor?

JOSH MORROW

Smells like something burning.

Jeff has a very intense expression.

JEFF MIDTOMAC

Flesh!

Dr. Lovette starts to feel uneasy.

DR. LOVETTE

OK, guys. Let's find a way out of here. I don't want to have to spend the night down here.

Everyone is in agreement, but as they prepare to go in search of a way out, they all suddenly stop, literally falling over one another.

SCENE 11: THE RESURRECTION OF FATHER DEMETRIC

DAMIAN LOVECRAFT

Oh…my…God!

FATHER DEMETRIC

God, indeed!

What stands before them is a sight no eyes should ever have to see. From the depths of hell, Father Demetric has returned. He looks as if he clawed his way out, raised above the ashes. Only horror films have been known to reflect this degree of terror. He stands at a distance but not far enough for these terrified observers. A tall, thin, and straight (as he always was) form he is wearing a dusty long black cassock with thirty-three buttons, which represent the years of the life of Jesus, the same one he wore when he was condemning souls to hell. He stands there silent, with an air of superiority, as if he knows he is free. His face and hands, which are the only visible parts, have a grayish tone, the color found on a corpse that has died from hypoxia. His face is long, narrow, and chiseled, and his eyes are sunken. His lips are dry and appear to be peeling, with scant traces of blood on them. And when he first speaks, his mouth exhales a great deal of dust, as if it has been accumulating over the last one hundred eighty years. His voice is deep and authoritative, as it was in life, but chilling and almost mechanical now.

FATHER DEMETRIC

Welcome…what took you so long?

The group can't take it any longer, so they all take off in the same direction, while assisting Kyle because of his injured leg.

FATHER DEMETRIC

Where are you going? You didn't meet the others. We've been waiting for you.

Then he breaks out into a sinister laugh. The harder he laughs the wider his mouth becomes and the more spats of blood there appear to be, especially in the corners of his mouth.

After running until they're almost breathless, ducking and turning around corners, they stop and take a breath. Everyone is barely able to speak.

JOSH MORROW

What in the hell is that?

KYLE QUENTIN

Do you think it's somebody in a costume playing a joke?

DAMIAN LOVECRAFT

Hell, no! He's obviously dead.

Samantha is shaking with terror.

SAMANTHA PRENTISS

That's not possible…is it?

Justine looks to Dr. Lovette for comfort.

JUSTINE COATES

I'm scared, Dr. Lovette.

DR. LOVETTE

I would be lying if I didn't say I felt the same. But we need to stay calm; we'll figure this out.

DAMIAN LOVECRAFT

Stay calm, Doctor? I'm having trouble keeping my legs under me. And what did it mean when it said, "We've been waiting for you?" And it mentioned the others. What others? What's going on?

DR. LOVETTE

I don't know, but I don't feel good about it.

JEFF MIDTOMAC

Whatever it is, we need to get as far away as possible. As we were running around, I noticed that this place seems to have several corridors going in all different directions. It's a large area, so we need to work hard and fast and furious to find a way out, hopefully before it catches up to us.

Everyone gathers together, but before they're able to flee, from nowhere appears Father Demetric again. Everyone panics and tries to leave, but at every turn, Father Demetric appears like magic and hinders their escape.

Dr. Lovette and Jeff realize escape is futile. So they stand in front of the students, shielding them as they're forced to endure Father Demetric's presence.

FATHER DEMETRIC

*For over one hundred eighty years, I have been
trapped in this world with these souls of the
damned. With the unworthy souls I ensured
would dwell here forever. In life I served God.
I condemned the impure, unholy, and unworthy. Down here I am God, and all shall serve
me.*

Dr. Lovette, who is still holding the book found in
the basement, clenches and looks down at it. As if his
words have triggered a thought.

The group continues to stand in sheer fright as Father
Demetric introduces them to the world they've entered and what's to follow.

FATHER DEMETRIC

*Here, as in life, I'm lord and master. Meet a
few of my unworthy minions.*

Father Demetric raises his arms in the air, and like
magic, on either side of him appear the most gruesome
beings, hideous in comparison to Father Demetric.
To his right are three condemned souls wearing rusty
chains around their necks attached to each other at the
neck, with the closest to Father Demetric attached to
his wrist. To his left are three more souls, attached in
the same manner with the closest attached to Father

Demetric's left wrist. Like a chain gang, he wears them attached to him as if they are accessories, each with a number branded into the forehead. It would appear they are slaves...and they understand this.

Dr. Lovette and the group continue to stand at attention, paralyzed with fear, unaware of what's to come and whether they'll ever get out of here alive. Dr. Lovette finally musters up the nerve to speak.

DR. LOVETTE

What is it you want? Please, we just want to leave here.

Dr. Lovette tries to appeal to its humanity, if there is indeed any. Father Demetric just laughs that awful sinister laugh. Then his tone changes and becomes harsh and forward.

FATHER DEMETRIC

Leave here? No one leaves here!

DR. LOVETTE

We just want to go home.

Father Demetric looks at Dr. Lovette with those sunken piercing eyes.

SCENE 12: FATHER DEMETRIC AND HIS MINIONS

FATHER DEMETRIC

Home? You are home.

He raises his arms again.

FATHER DEMETRIC

Just ask them.

The members of Dr. Lovette's group are becoming more and more terrified, but they realize there's nothing they can do. So they continue to endure his presence and intimidation.

FATHER DEMETRIC

Meet "the souls of the damned." Condemned souls, not fit for consecrated ground.

The group is horrified.

Father Demetric looks to his right side, to the far end. At the very end is condemned soul number 231, the "surgeon." Graduate of one of the first medical colleges in the country, in Williamsburg, Virginia. He appears normal in human form, but it is what's underneath that makes him so sinister. The doctor was considered distinguished, handsome some might say, though that observation is quite the contrary now. Just a ghostly gray image of his former self. Instead of the look of a distinguished physician, he more resembles an eighteenth-century butcher. Disheveled, wearing blood-stained garments, he stands there with a look of superiority.

Father Demetric formally introduces him.

FATHER DEMETRIC

I give you the "surgeon."

As those words roll off Father Demetric's tongue, the surgeon reveals what earned him a position in one of the niches of hell. He swings open his upper garment, and what they see has the group gasp. Attached and impinged to his flesh, from neck to waist is a frightening array of surgical tools used during the seventeenth and eighteenth century. This assortment consists of a curved amputation knife, used to cut through skin, muscle, and bone. The cervical dilator was used to dilate the cervix during labor…my how he enjoyed that. The surgeon has many more items on his "flesh arsenal" such as a scarifying instrument, used to pierce the skin for bloodletting.

124

This procedure was believed to cure and prevent illness and disease. And the trephine, a hand-powered drill used to perforate the skull. These are only a few of the unsightly metal contraptions he wears.

FATHER DEMETRIC

In this world, unlike on earth, I appreciate the doctor's skills. And young girls, it was with them that his best work was performed.

He exhales a chilling laugh.

The surgeon's crimes were some of the most heinous ever documented in medical history, but he was never tried. Though he did not spend a day in jail or the asylum, nor did he receive the guillotine, he was never allowed to practice medicine again. Because of the culture during this period, his crimes were concealed. This decision was influenced by some sort of misguided belief that a doctor's position was one of status, unlike the others who were just mere common folk. Therefore the surgeon was confined to his premises under house arrest, never to practice medicine again, reputation intact, enjoying the spoils of life. Upon his death, unlike in life, the "surgeon" was no better than the common folk and was placed in the wall of the damned, number 231.

Father Demetric's stare moves from the "surgeon" to the soul in the middle. There stands the very first installer into the wall of the damned, number 1, the "whore." She presents with a nervous twitch, consistently, slightly moving, which annoys Father Demetric. He commands her.

FATHER DEMETRIC

Still, whore.

Father Demetric address the group.

FATHER DEMETRIC

Our first resident to be placed in the wall, the "whore" is the worst of the worst, a severe menace to society. Without a moral compass to guide her, and a reputation to perform the most deviant sexual acts, she is a perfect fit for the wall. She was willing to perform services to anyone, anywhere, for any price. This one has been known to service patrons in alleyways, ditches, and her most heinous…graveyards, consecrated ground, rumor has it.

She's wearing a thin, dingy, tattered slip, almost see-through. She is emaciated, her bone structure protruding from beneath her pale, toneless skin. Her teeth are decayed and rotten, the result of lack of calcium and protein. Her eyes are sunken with profound black rings around them. Her lips cracked and dry, her hair brittle, dry and thin, most of which has fallen out. There

126

is only a patch of hair left here or there, the scalp so dry with eczema or something worse. Impaired balance, apparent blindness in left eye, and madness, all three classic characteristics of syphilis. A sexually transmitted disease no doubt acquired during her years of ill repute. Though in her poor crippled mind, she's enticing and alluring. She was considered a throwaway of society, and according to Father Demetric, a forbidden child of God.

Beaten, mistreated, as well as emotionally and physically abused in her life, this wayward soul fell to the mercy of Father Demetric, but there would be no mercy, just a cold unconsecrated niche within a stone wall. Branded not only on her forehead but also on her back, buttocks, and behind her legs, she wears the grid marks of the iron crib used to place the body into the oven in the crematorium. When on Father Demetric's commend, she turns to reveal this horrific sight, members of the group gasp, but Father Demetric laughs, as does a few of his minions, including the "whore" herself.

Directly chained to Father Demetric's wrist is the "weeping mother" and the "stillborn child," number 10.

FATHER DEMETRIC

A bastard conceived out of wedlock, both sinners, mother and child. Neither fit for consecrated ground.

127

The lifeless mother stands there in rags weeping for her dead child she's cuddling in her arms. The child's face is not visible, it's snuggly wrapped in a filthy blanket. Not a word does she utter; she simply weeps for her lost. The mother was a widow, but according to Father Demetric's vile tongue, the child was born out of wedlock and immediately following the birth of her stillborn, she died. So they were placed in the wall of the damned together; one urn, one niche.

Samantha can't take it any longer and her fear gets the best of her. She takes off running; the others follow.

Father Demetric starts to laugh, as does some of his minions.

FATHER DEMETRIC

We've just gotten started.

Once everyone catches up to Samantha and tries to console her, Father Demetric reappears, slaves at his side.

The entire group is terrified. Samantha, with tears pouring, pleads.

SAMANTHA PRENTISS

Please let us out of here. I just want to go home.

Samantha notices the "whore" leering at her. Father Demetric responds.

FATHER DEMETRIC

Leave? But there is still so much more for you to see.

Father Demetric looks to his left side, to the far end. Sitting on the floor, in stocks, is condemned soul number 400, the "transgressor." Father Demetric particularly harbored a hatred for this poor soul. Rumors, innuendos, and Father Demetric's own prejudice is what earned the "transgressor" a niche in the wall of the damned.

FATHER DEMETRIC

Here before you is a disgrace to mankind. His crime? He looked to men for his pleasures and sexual satisfaction...so I'm told. A sin he should have been hanged for, but I decided on a punishment that was much more appropriate. Just look at him, his mouth in particular; one can only imagine where it's been.

Now Justine breaks down.

JUSTINE COATES

Stop it, please stop it.

Father Demetric angrily responds.

FATHER DEMETRIC

Silence!

As Father Demetric verbally abuses the "transgressor," he continues sitting, head dropped, ankles in the stocks Father Demetric enslaved him in when alive. When Father Demetric looked at the "transgressor," he saw what he considered a vile creature, one of questionable sexuality. Once the rumors and accusations of the "transgressor's" alleged sexual preference started, most of which were spread by Father Demetric, he became an outcast. It is unknown whether or not this rumor was the result of a confession or Father Demetric's malice. In any event, once he was on Father Demetric's hate list, fact or fiction, it was over for him.

After years of residing in unsanitary conditions and crowded quarters such as almshouses, reformatories, houses of refuge, shelters, and prisons, the "transgressor" fell victim to consumption, or pulmonary tuberculosis, as it is known today. He probably had a poor constitution, the effect of being undernourished and having a compromised immune system. The poor thing, ravished by the disease, wore the look of consumption, with a progressive wasting away of his entire body. He contracted kwashiorkor—depicted in his distended abdomen—the result of malnutrition. His skin was pasty white, and he lost all of his teeth.

He developed a persistent cough so forceful you could literally hear his ribs crack. In rags, with no shoes, the "transgressor's" punishment was that his legs be placed in stocks and that he be imprisoned, only allowed food and drink on Father Demetric's command. For several hours a day, Father Demetric would have him placed in the courtyard for all to see. Attached to his back was a sign that read, *Do Not Feed Animal.* For two years this poor soul endured this humiliation, with scraps of food thrown to him, mostly by passers-by and those who took pity on him. He suffered with hunger, disease, and squalor for the remainder of his days. It is said that as the "transgressor" was approaching the end of life, he cried out to Father Demetric for last rites, but he was denied.

Now Father Demetric moves on to the middle. There stands the one who would appear to be the most innocent of all. But according to Father Demetric...

FATHER DEMETRIC

This one appears innocent on the outside, but on the inside, I assure you, he earned his niche in the wall.

Father Demetric is referring to condemned soul number 332, "Fire Boy," as he is amply named.

131

FATHER DEMETRIC

The poor parents of this hopeless child prayed day after day that he would be redeemed. I prayed with them. But once sin settled into the soul of this one, redemption was no longer an option.

The eight-year-old boy with burns on his face, wearing burned and smoky seventeenth-century school garments, always had problems, particularly with starting fires. He would start fires in hayfields, cornfields, and barns, just to see them burn. No one is sure if it was the colors, flicker of lights, or the destruction it caused that attracted this community menace, as he was considered. One day at the little wooden schoolhouse he attended, a fire broke out. No one got out alive, not even the school pet. Everything and everyone perished...even "Fire Boy" himself. Everyone blamed "Fire boy" for starting the fire.

Although his guilt was never proven, his history with starting fires contributed to the communities' decision to cast the blame on him. Father Demetric was in agreement to this decision. Therefore, his remains were considered unfit for consecrated ground. This was a decision Father Demetric passed down, but it was fully supported by the parents and family of those who perished. "Fire Boy's" parents pleaded with Father Demetric, but it fell on deaf ears.

FATHER DEMETRIC

As you can see, even for the young, there's a place in hell.

The last condemned soul directly chained to Father Demetric's wrist is the "thief/murderer," number 35.

FATHER DEMETRIC

This wretched soul died at the gallows...a public hanging. If ever a vile creature deserved such a death, it was this one, wearing the clothes and shoes he stole from his victims. Oh yes, this was a nasty one.

There are those who said the punishment fit the crime and that the placement of his remains in the wall following his execution...just. Fat, greedy, and grotesque, he often robbed and murdered those he befriended. His sinister crimes went on for years, on and off, as his needs arrived, which made it difficult to catch him. Father Demetric's actions in this case, in reference to both the execution and the columbarium wall, seemed to soften the blow for those he unjustly condemned. Many people saw this case as a way of balancing the scales.

FATHER DEMETRIC

Now that you've met the others...

He raises his arms to the air, the chains still connected to each of them.

FATHER DEMETRIC

...join us.

He breaks into his skin-crawling laugh. In Father Demetric's distorted mind all of mankind are sinners and deserve to be a part of the wall of the damned. Everyone in the group takes off running in several different directions, some alone, some together. Then the chains connecting the souls drop to the floor, even those attached to Father Demetric.

FATHER DEMETRIC

Go, my minions, go and bring me the souls of the unworthy. Failure, and your suffering will echo throughout centuries to come.

Father Demetric's minions fade away and eventually so does he.

SCENE 13: JUSTINE ON HER OWN AND DESPERATE

Justine is separated from the rest of the group, terrified, and all alone. The sublevel is huge. Once separated it could be some time before she comes across the others in the group. She frantically runs around, without direction. There are no designated rooms, just corridors of open space, which appear to lead nowhere. She's briskly walking backward, forward, sideways, calling out to the group.

JUSTINE COATES

Dr. Lovette, Kyle, Damian, anyone, where are you? Oh, my God, will someone please answer me? I'm afraid.

Then she tries to convince herself to calm down by analyzing the situation logically.

JUSTINE COATES

OK, calm down, Justine. This cannot be happening. Dead souls, ghosts, whatever, do not exist. This has to be some kind of game, a very bad joke, a mass hallucination, anything but what has occurred here today. OK, I'll just try and find the others and get the hell out of here.

As she turns around to go look for the others, directly in front of her is the soul of the "surgeon." She stands there staring at it, horrified, afraid to make a move. She stares up and down, only getting a glance of the ghastly tools on its body. She's so frightened she can't take her eyes off them. Then it speaks.

SURGEON

Which procedure do you require?

He widens his garment, revealing his "flesh arsenal" of tools. Justine starts to tremble and shake all over. Then she breaks out in a howling scream and takes off running. Others from the group, who are also separated, are able to hear her screams but are unable to pinpoint where they're coming from. The others call out to her and to each other, but to no avail. Justine tries to escape, but at every twist and turn, the "surgeon" appears. She's exhausted and weak with fear, so she submits to the fact that she's at his mercy. In a corner is an old surgical table, which appears from nowhere.

Justine, who had been standing, is now magically on the table, strapped down. The "surgeon" is in a chair setting next to her.

SURGEON

Tell me, young lady, what ails you?

Justine is screaming, crying, and pleading to be released.

SURGEON

Hush, don't fret now. I've done these procedures hundreds of times.

The "surgeon" is looking forward to getting back to work after being out of commission for over a century and a half. His first patient, being a young lady, pleases him. Young girls were his specialty. In his chair, he rolls to the end of the table and puts his diabolic plan to work.

SURGEON

Let's see what we have here.

Justine shivers from the touch of his ghastly hands, which feel like a cold whisper as they glide across her skin. As he spreads her legs, each one falls off the edge of the cold steel surgical table. From his flesh arsenal, he twists, turns, and pulls the vaginal speculum from his flesh. The "surgeon" has been known to use this device to probe various body cavities and orifices. Justine is weeping and praying. She's so afraid and exhausted that she faints.

SURGEON

Now, now, just relax, you won't feel a thing.

As the "surgeon" utters these words, though still restrained, Justine's entire body goes into a full-extension spasm, as if electricity is flowing through her, like *Frankenstein's* monster. The "surgeon" is at work, and he's enjoying his trade.

SURGEON

Oops, did that hurt?

He laughs.

The "surgeon" has used the vaginal speculum to perform an exploratory procedure. He jams the speculum into Justine and uses the crank to expand the area, ripping into the vaginal wall. She screams from the pain he's inflicting on her.

SURGEON

OK, let's see if your baby is ready to be born.

JUSTINE

No, stop! I'm not having a baby. Please stop. You're killing me!

The "surgeon" rips the cervical dilator from his flesh. He then dives into her cervix and dilates the device beyond the measurements on the scale, resulting in profound tearing and profuse bleeding. Justine screams and cries as her tormentor continues to work. She is pale and cold, and she is fading fast. She stares out into space, and in a low, solemn tone, she says...

JUSTINE COATES

I'm dying.

As her blood drips to the floor, she turns her face to the side, as not to be facing her executioner. The life begins to float out of Justine's body. The "surgeon," without any remorse, simply says...

SURGEON

No baby here!

He laughs and slowly disappears.

SCENE 14: WARREN APPEALS TO ONE OF THE SOULS

Warren has been wandering around alone for some time also. He, too, is able to hear the others, but like Justine, is unable to find them. He looks down a corridor and is able to see someone or something on the floor, from a distance. He's as afraid as the others, but he decides that if it's one of his classmates, Dr. Lovette, or Jeff, it's worth the risk, so he reaches out.

WARREN SYKES

Hello, who's down there?

There's no response, so he proceeds down the corridor, moving in closer.

WARREN SYKES

Hey, Josh, is that you? Kyle, Damian, anyone? Who's there?

There's still no response, so Warren continues down the corridor but very cautiously. As he gets closer, he realizes it's one of the souls. But he does not feel threatened, so he proceeds carefully.

WARREN SYKES

You're the "transgressor," aren't you?

The "transgressor" is still in the sitting position, with his ankles bounded in the stocks. He just sits there looking down, doesn't utter a word. Warren tries to appeal to him.

WARREN SYKES

Look, my friends and I just want to find a way out of here...what's going on here?

Warren raises his voice.

WARREN SYKES

Please, we just want to get out of here. We want to go home...Would you please help us?

Warren's words seem to move the "transgressor." He looks up and appears to be trying to speak. Perhaps he is going to tell him a way out or to simply damn him. He doesn't find out, because Father Demetric appears and reminds the "transgressor" who's in charge.

FATHER DEMETRIC

You dare defy me!

The "transgressor" is terrified, shaking his head, indicating no.

FATHER DEMETRIC

Your suffering will be merciless.

Warren does not hang around to find out what Father Demetric's intentions are for the "transgressor." He takes off running and never looks back.

SCENE 15: KYLE QUENTIN AND HIS ANTICS

After running around like the others, Kyle finds himself back near the columbarium wall and the stairs leading up to the basement, where out of nowhere appears the "thief/murderer." Kyle, whose leg is still in a lot of pain from his injury, staggers to keep a distance between them by consistently moving around.

KYLE QUENTIN

What do you want? Look, I don't want any trouble. I just want to get out of here. Do you understand?

The condemned soul just stands there smiling, exposing his revolting grin. Kyle is becoming increasingly uneasy and intimidated by this soul. He tries using humor to calm his nerves.

KYLE QUENTIN

Hey, what about the two of us getting together after we get out of here? I know of a really

*good dentist. You may be able to get some work
done, pro bono.*

Kyle has been consistently moving this entire time
and has found himself at the bottom of the stairs leading back up to the basement. Kyle continues shooting
the breeze as he ascends the thirty steps on his buttocks, lifting and carrying his injured leg.

Although reaching the top of the stairs will only gain
him entry to the trapped basement, it's a hell of a lot
better than where he is now. Kyle has reached the top
of the stairs. He's tired but feeling pretty confident
that he's at a safe distance.

KYLE QUENTIN

*OK, I'm happy to say, this is where we go our
separate ways. I'm free.*

The "thief/murderer" points to the top of the stairs.
And with a twist of the wrist, Kyle's entire body is
flipped to the prone position, face down. Kyle is unable
to move. The "thief/murderer" is in complete control.
With Kyle's chin directly on the edge of the cold stone
step, the soul makes a tight fist and pulls Kyle's body
down the steps at a rapid speed. Feet first, his chin hits
the edge of every step as he's yanked down the stairs.
By the time he hits the bottom, he's almost decapitat-
ed, his head hanging on a piece of skin, relaxing on his
upper back. The thief takes Kyle's shoes off his feet.

SCENE 16: SAMANTHA MEETS HER MATCH

Samantha is shivering cold, sobbing, and afraid. She's spooked by everything, even the sound of her own footsteps. She's barely holding on.

She is crying.

SAMANTHA PRENTISS

I want to go home. I shouldn't be here. Please help me, someone.

She drops to the floor.

She hears a wicked laugh, which startles her. She looks up and sees the "whore" jerking and laughing hysterically, while running her fingers through her scant patches of hair. Samantha should jump to her feet and run, but she's much too tired to do so. So down on her hands and knees she begs not to be harmed.

SAMANTHA PRENTISS

Please, please don't hurt me, I'll do anything.

The "whore" is pleased, and smiles. Phrases such as "I'll do anything" and "What do you like?" excite her. These are words she's spoken often. Then she puts her nasty little mind to work. Unable to complete sentences, only short phases, she gets her point across.

WHORE

You and me, girly, we work, make money. I show you.

Samantha looks confused.

WHORE

We do men, you know…open legs.

Then she makes an obscene gesture with her mouth and breaks into a wicked laugh. Samantha is so appalled she spits at the "whore" and lashes out.

SAMANTHA PRENTISS

You're cheap and disgusting, I'm nothing like you. You're nothing but trash, pure trash.

The "whore" is no longer laughing.

SAMANTHA PRENTISS

No good, you, me, the same.

The "whore" believes she and Samantha are kindred souls. She wants Samantha to take a good look at herself. The "whore" points to a wall, where a mirror appears. And as anyone would do, Samantha looks into the mirror. It is just like in the fairy tale, when the evil queen sees her true reflection in the mirror. So it is for Samantha. What the whore sees is a reflection of Samantha; what Samantha sees is a hideous creature, a version of the "whore." The "whore's" work is done, and she succeeds at getting into Samantha's head. Between the fright, despair, and any hope of finding a way out, Samantha breaks. And with head and face first, she runs and crashes into the mirror, which turns out to have been an illusion. What she really crashes into is a stone wall. The "whore" is satisfied. All of Samantha's beauty is gone.

SCENE 17: DR. LOVETTE AND JEFF SEARCH FOR THE OTHERS

Dr. Lovette and Jeff manage to not have been separated. They have been exploring the corridors, desperately trying to find a way out, as well as searching for the others. They are discussing the situation they're in and trying to figure a way out.

DR. LOVETTE

Is this really happening? Or is it just a bad dream?

JEFF MIDTOMAC

I'm sorry to say it's really happening.

DR. LOVETTE

All of this is my fault. First I bring my students on this trip, then I get caught in the emotion and end up down here in what turns out to be hell.

Jeff consoles Dr. Lovette.

JEFF MIDTOMAC

Look, no one could ever have foreseen any-thing like this happening, or even imagined it possible.

DR. LOVETTE

I just feel so responsible and so powerless. If we could just figure out what we're up against, we may have a chance of making it out of here.

Dr. Lovette and Jeff are able to hear someone approaching, running very fast. They don't know who or what to expect. It's Warren Sykes. Dr. Lovette is thrilled to see him. She embraces him.

DR. LOVETTE

Thank God. Are you all right? Did you see any of the others?

WARREN SYKES

No, I didn't see any of the others. I was able to hear voices, but I was unable to make out where they were coming from.

DR. LOVETTE

It was the same for us.

WARREN SYKES

But I came across one of those things we saw earlier.

Dr. Lovette gasped.

DR. LOVETTE

Did it hurt you? Or try to do anything to you?

WARREN SYKES

No. It was the one called the "transgressor." It just sat there on the floor looking down, not a word. So when it didn't appear hostile, I started talking, appealing to it for help. It seemed it might work until its master showed up.

JEFF MIDTOMAC

What happened then?

WARREN SYKES

I don't know. I took off and didn't look back.

DR. LOVETTE

Just before you showed up, I'd said that if we can figure out what we're up against our chances of getting out of here may improve.

Warren points at something.

WARREN SYKES

What about that?

Warren is referring to the book from the basement which Dr. Lovette is still holding.

DR. LOVETTE

Yes, "Souls of the Damned." You know we never did open this.

Dr. Lovette is thinking.

JEFF MIDTOMAC

What is it?

DR. LOVETTE

Remember when the first one appeared, it said, "Meet the Souls of the Damned?" Well it's no coincidence that the title of this book, and those "condemned souls," as they were referred to, have something in common.

JEFF MIDTOMAC

Are you thinking what I'm thinking?

DR. LOVETTE

That some of the answers we're looking for are in this book.

WARREN SYKES

There's only one way to find out.

DR. LOVETTE

Here goes!

The book is very old and fragile and could damage easily. So Dr. Lovette patiently and cautiously opens the book to the first page and reads the inscription.

DR. LOVETTE

"Here in this unconsecrated wall lie the remains of evil, may their souls never wander this earth again."

Hearing the words out loud induces fright in them. Jeff states the obvious.

JEFF MIDTOMAC

This isn't good.

Dr. Lovette turns the page and comes across what turns out to be an account of all Father Demetric's crimes... at least those that were known. Dr. Lovette responds solemnly.

DR. LOVETTE

Oh, boy!

WARREN SYKES

What is it?

DR. LOVETTE

I'd say a meticulous account of the wall.

WARREN SYKES

You're saying that those things came from that wall?

DR. LOVETTE

It's starting to look that way.

Jeff agrees with Dr. Lovette.

JEFF MIDTOMAC

I think she's on to something. Take a look here. There are pages upon pages of entries, starting in 1804. Remember that piece of faceplate your student found that had the number 1 and 1804 on it? Well, according to the entry here, number 1, 1804, is the whore. Look, first column name (whore), next column number (1); she's the first. Over in the next column is the date (1804) and the last column, crimes and sins (whore, prostitute, fornication).

WARREN SYKES

This can't be happening.

JEFF MIDTOMAC

There's not much room for doubt.

DR. LOVETTE

What about the others? Either of you remember their numbers? What they were called?

WARREN SYKES

Sure. The one I came across was called the "transgressor," number 400.

Dr. Lovette fingers through the pages.

DR. LOVETTE

Here we are. Transgressor, number 400, date 1822, crimes/sins: homosexuality, sin against the church. What about the others?

JEFF MIDTOMAC

I can remember some of the other numbers. Numbers 231, 332...and now I'm drawing a blank on the other one.

DR. LOVETTE

It's OK. Let's fine these two. Here's number 231, the "surgeon," crimes/sins: heinous surgical procedures; and number 332, "Fire Boy," started a fire in schoolhouse, everything and everyone perished, including him.

JEFF MIDTOMAC

Oh, I remember the other one now, number 35.

DR. LOVETTE

Oh, that was the "murderer." I remember that one. Number 35. I'll have to go back toward the front. OK, I found it, "thief/murderer." This one's crimes/sins are pretty self-explanatory. Followed victims, often befriending, then robbing, murdering. Sometimes murdering, then robbing.

JEFF MIDTOMAC

But we don't know who this "Lord" and "Master" is, as he referred to himself.

Dr. Lovette is thinking again.

WARREN SYKES

What is it?

DR. LOVETTE

I remember in researching the history of the church, I came across some information pertaining to the missionary priest who led the Roman Catholic colony here. I don't recall his name, but I remember reading how instrumental he was in the building of the church. I remember thinking there wasn't much information on him, just those couple of facts...I can't remember much more, only that he died in 1829. Now that I think of that piece of faceplate I found, it was dated 1829, and though I was unable to make out the number, the word "Father" was right beneath the date.

WARREN SYKES

Are you saying a Roman Catholic priest is buried down here?

The three just stand there looking at one another.

JEFF MIDTOMAC

Again, there's only one way to find out.

160

Dr. Lovette goes to the back of the book to the last entry. They find what they're looking for.

DR. LOVETTE

Here it is. Father Demetric, Missionary Priest (pioneer), number 413, date 1829.

Dr. Lovette pauses and looks up.

DR. LOVETTE

Well, this confirms my date. The list of crimes/sins against him consist of unlawful imprisonment, denial of last rites, false/questionable accusations against citizens, prejudicial behavior, and denial of consecrated ground.

The three of them look at one another. Dr. Lovette responds in a solemn tone.

DR. LOVETTE

It's him! He played judge and juror with these people's souls. Those who did not live by his laws or commands were sentenced to this wall. This wall is a testament that hell really does exist…and Father Demetric…is its devil.

JEFF MIDTOMAC

Well, at least we know what we're up against. But how does this information help with getting out of here?

DR. LOVETTE

I don't know yet but it could be helpful with survival until we can escape.

WARREN SYKES

Do you really believe that? The part about getting out of here, with everything we've seen here?

Dr. Lovette places her hand on Warren's arm.

DR. LOVETTE

Don't give up. We're going to get out of here.

Jeff comes across some very interesting information on the last few pages of the book.

JEFF MIDTOMAC

Hey, take a look at this. There's an inscription at the top of the page. It reads, "I hereby name thee 'Keeper of the Souls,' Father Augustus, in the year of our Lord and Heavenly Father, eighteen hundred and twenty nine." And that tree, just below the inscription looks like some kind of genealogy or something.

DR. LOVETTE

Actually, it's a family tree. Check out the name on the first branch at the top... Sebastian Domitianus (1829), and the descending branches, Sebastian Domitianus, II (1879), Sebastian Domitianus, III (1919), Sebastian Domitianus, IV (1954)...

Dr. Lovette pauses.

DR. LOVETTE

...and Sebastian Domitianus, V (1988).

She looks up at Jeff and Warren as if a light went on in her head. And it would appear Jeff is on the same wavelength.

DR. LOVETTE

Could this just be a coincidence?

JEFF MIDTOMAC

I don't know. How old would you say Sebastian is?

DR. LOVETTE

Hard to say but I'd guess fifty-six, fifty-seven.

Warren catches on.

WARREN SYKES

That handyman we met earlier…Sebastian. Are you saying this is his genealogy?

JEFF MIDTOMAC

Kinda looks that way.

WARREN SYKES

But these dates…no way was he born in 1988.

DR. LOVETTE

No, I don't think these dates represent births. Notice the first date is 1829. The same year Father Demetric was placed down here. The dates on the tree range anywhere from thirty-four to fifty years apart. No, what I think these dates represent is the passing of this book down the family line. From one generation to the next.

Dr. Lovette has a serious expression.

JEFF MIDTOMAC

What is it?

DR. LOVETTE

I'm remembering something Sebastian said when he was standing in the entryway of the church. He said "Many, many years ago, my great-great-great-grandfather was handed a responsibility, which he handed to his son, and he to his son, until it reached me."

WARREN SYKES

You mean he knew those things were down here and he didn't warn us?

DR. LOVETTE

No, no, no. He tried. We just didn't listen.

As these facts are unfolding, Sebastian is in the rectory on bended knees praying.

SCENE 18: SEBASTIAN IN THE RECTORY

Sebastian is praying in his Roman ancestor's dialect/
tongue. With eyes shut tight, he is praying so intense-
ly, squeezing his crucifix so tight, that the four points
impinge on his flesh. As the blood drains down his
arm and drops to the floor, Sebastian looks to God for
answers. This is a testament of faith...a true believ-
er. Sebastian stops praying and opens his eyes. And as
touched by God he says...

SEBASTIAN

I know what I must do!

SCENE 19: JOSH IN THE DARK

Josh, who credits himself as adventurous, fearless, and up for anything, finds himself at a loss and as terrified as the others. Stumbling and tripping he finds himself in an area with the least amount of lighting. He is unable to see his hands right in front of him. But lucky for him, or perhaps unlucky, he's wearing a neon green glow-in-the-dark nylon jacket. At first he fumbles around. Then, as if blind, he uses the cold stone wall as his guide.

JOSH MORROW

Where in the hell am I? I can't see a damn thing. Hello! Can anyone hear me? I have to get out of here. I don't want to die down here. OK, if I use this wall and walk adjacent to it, perhaps it will lead me to the others or at least some lighting.

SCENE 20: DR. LOVETTE, JEFF, AND WARREN RECEIVE A VISITOR

Dr. Lovette closes the book.

DR. LOVETTE

Well, this book has given us a pretty good idea of all the souls we've come across, including where Sebastian comes in.

JEFF MIDTOMAC

Not quite. We missed one or two.

Jeff is alluding to the weeping "mother and stillborn child" standing at a distance. They suddenly appear from nowhere but do not seem threatening. Dr. Lovette wants to attempt communication with the soul. Jeff and Warren are opposed to this. But she will not be deterred.

SCENE 21: JOSH SMELLS SMOKE

Josh is trying to find his way out of the darkness, but does not appear to be getting anywhere. He's just going around in circles, though he's not fully aware of this but suspects.

JOSH MORROW

Let me rest. I feel as if I've been going in circles.

He stands there taking in deep breaths. Then he senses something. He starts to sniff the air, stops, then sniffs some more.

JOSH MORROW

I smell something in here...it's smoke. Who's there?

He's on the move again in hopes of avoiding the smoke he smells.

SCENE 22: DR. LOVETTE REACHES OUT

Against Jeff and Warren's wishes, Dr. Lovette proceeds with her quest of reaching out to the "weeping mother."

Dr. Lovette slowly and cautiously approaches.

WARREN SYKES

Be careful!

She nods.

DR. LOVETTE

Hi…my name is Leslie. Can you tell me your name?

She receives no response just continued weeping.

DR. LOVETTE

What about your baby? Does it have a name?

No response. Dr. Lovette moves in a little closer.

JEFF MIDTOMAC

Careful!

Dr. Lovette uses the maternal approach.

DR. LOVETTE

I would really love to see your baby.

As the "weeping mother" turns in Dr. Lovette's direction, the blanket opens at the top, revealing the stillborn child. It's horrifying, and Warren turns away. Dr. Lovette is able to hold her composure. Jeff has seen the remains of many children and babies in his line of work. So he's calm.

Jeff gives Warren a piece of advice.

JEFF MIDTOMAC

Pull it together. This may take a while.

SCENE 23: JOSH SENSES HE'S NOT ALONE

The smell of smoke is getting stronger and closer. Josh senses that the source of the smell is near him...in fact, even right in front of him. He grows more frightened and is tempted to reach out and try to feel what's there, but he dare not.

JOSH MORROW

Who's there? Answer me! Dammit, who's there, I said?

The smoke is so strong and thick now that he starts coughing. He cushions his back up against the cold stone wall. Josh staggers along the wall trying to escape the smoke, still unable to find his way. When it appears that he is consumed by the smoke and has given up, the smoke starts to thin. As this is unfolding, standing directly in front of him is a clear view of "Fire Boy." "Fire Boy" reaches out and touches Josh's jacket. And as touched by the hand of hell the nylon jacket starts to melt. Josh starts running and screaming as the rest of his garments melt.

SCENE 24: DR. LOVETTE, JEFF, AND WARREN REACT TO SCREAMS

As Dr. Lovette is attempting to communicate with the "weeping mother," which seems to be in vain, they hear screaming in the distance. Not knowing which student it is, they take off in the direction of the distress.

SCENE 25: JOSH DISAPPEARS

Josh's running now turns to a walk, as he's now dropping pieces of melted skin, until nothing is left but a skeleton, which simply drops to the ground…the adventure is over.

SCENE 26: BACK AT THE COLUMBARIUM WALL

After running around trying to find who was apparently in trouble, Dr. Lovette, Jeff, and Warren end up at the columbarium wall. Father Demetric and his minions greet them. The "surgeon," "whore," "thief/murderer," "Fire Boy," and "weeping mother and still-born child" are all present. The "transgressor" is also there, whose lips Father Demetric has wired together, as punishment for his defiance. On the floor is a slab with the bodies of the four slain students lying on it.

The three are horrified by the ghastly sight. Dr. Lovette, crying, lashes out.

DR. LOVETTE

You monsters, murderous monsters, what have you done? Why have you done this?

Jeff and Warren bring her back closer to them. She weakens in their arms. For the first time, Dr. Lovette's tender side is revealed.

Father Demetric points to the columbarium wall.

FATHER DEMETRIC

This is where they belong. This is where all sinners belong.

The very same furnace commissioned in 1804, starting with the whore, suddenly appears. Father Demetric waves his hand, and flames appear in the oven. Upon his command, the bodies, one by one, will go through the flames, ashes into urns, and placed in niches.

With arms raised in the air, Father Demetric commands the others to join him.

FATHER DEMETRIC

Come, join your friends. Soon you will come to realize what another has already accepted… it's inevitable.

The three survivors look at each other, baffled by this comment when, from behind Father Demetric, Damian steps out. They are stunned. Dr. Lovette fears he is in danger.

DR. LOVETTE

Damian, come, run! Get away from it.

Damian just stands there. Jeff states what is now the obvious.

JEFF MIDTOMAC

He's not coming.

Dr. Lovette is confused.

DAMIAN LOVECRAFT

When he came after me, I knew I didn't have the guts and was too cowardly to fight. So instead I made an offer, and he accepted.

DR. LOVETTE

What are you talking about?

DAMIAN LOVECRAFT

I pleaded with him to spare my life, and I shall be his human servant. I will follow his every command, sworn to honor and obey his every wish. I've never been very religious, but you must admit this is the only God ever seen on earth.

WARREN SYKES

You've completely lost your mind.

DAMIAN LOVECRAFT

Sykes, I've always hated you.

He turns to Father Demetric.

DAMIAN LOVECRAFT

Let him be the first to go through the flames.

FATHER DEMETRIC

First, those who are already prepared…

Father Demetric looks to the bodies.

FATHER DEMETRIC

…then the others.

He looks to Dr. Lovette, Jeff, and Warren.

The three remaining survivors simply stand there with nowhere to run and nowhere to hide.

SCENE 27: SEBASTIAN BEGINS HIS QUEST

Back at the rectory, Sebastian stands in the doorway holding what would normally take two or more to carry...the Holy Tabernacle. The storm that had been forecasted earlier has started. Torrential rains and gusting winds begin, but Sebastian knows his mission and will not be deterred. Weak and sick, Sebastian staggers out of the doorway carrying the weighted Holy Tabernacle, as Jesus carried the cross. He continues his quest through high winds and heavy rains. He begins praying in his ancestor's dialect.

SCENE 28: FATHER DEMETRIC COMMANDS

Father Demetric commands his minions to place the bodies, one at a time on the crib. Dr. Lovette lashes out.

DR. LOVETTE

Stop it, you monster. You can't do this.

FATHER DEMETRIC

Silence! Your time will come.

Father Demetric points to Kyle's body first. They obey and place his body on the crib.

SCENE 29: SEBASTIAN AT THE CHURCH ENTRYWAY

Sebastian makes it to the church entryway. He walks down the aisle, and halfway down his legs can no longer hold him and he falls, as did Jesus while carrying the cross. But as Jesus got back on his feet and carried on, so does Sebastian. He continues his journey, enduring the weight of the Tabernacle, praying all the way.

SCENE 30: INTO THE FIRE

The oven door is open. Father Demetric nods his head, and the souls lift the crib, with Kyle's body, and proceed toward the furnace. Dr. Lovette is determined to stop this but Jeff and Warren hold her back. They can only stand and hopelessly watch.

SCENE 31: SEBASATIAN MAKES IT TO THE ALTAR

Sebastian has reached the end of his journey. Adjacent to the altar is the column that endured the weight of the Holy Tabernacle for over 225 years. Sebastian gently places the Holy Tabernacle on the floor as he pulls a chair to the column. He reaches to the floor and picks up the Holy Tabernacle. While standing on the chair with all his might, he places it atop the column as he recites the consecration ritual. Though consecrations are performed by a bishop, God had granted Sebastian the wisdom. For when the consecrated Tabernacle is present, all things within the structure are under its law. As Jesus Christ hung nailed to the cross at the end of his life, Sebastian clings to the column, which supports the Holy Tabernacle at the end of his. He can rest now…his work is done.

SCENE 32: THEY ARE PULLED BACK

As Kyle's body is about to be placed in the oven, Father Demetric and the six souls cease and desist. They are alarmed and sense something is happening, something that only they are aware of. Some of the souls are antsy, and they scatter. They flitter about, worried. "Weeping mother" and the "transgressor" appear content, while the others appear frightened. Father Demetric shouts…

FATHER DEMETRIC

No!

The church starts to shake and shift. The cracks in the walls, as a result of the deconsecration, appear to be mending, as if repairing themselves.

The souls are being pulled back into the wall. Evil is no match for the power of the Holy Tabernacle. Father Demetric and the souls are comprised of ash, which slowly starts to dissipate. It is said that God made man from dirt, and upon death, to the dirt he returns.

As for these souls…it is to ash that they return. As the ash disperses, particles flow to the floor. Many of them, including Father Demetric, try and resist, but the power of the Tabernacle is too great.

As this is unfolding, the survivors look to the "transgressor" for the way out. Just as the ghost of "Christmas yet to come" could not speak but simply point, so does the "transgressor," with his head down and mouth wired. He points to an area on a nearby wall and smiles as he slowly dissipates, he is free. It is an area that is weak due to the torrential rain. Water is seeping in and running down the wall, which is mostly mud. The survivors start clawing and digging away at the soil at the top of the wall. Across the room, most of the souls have completely dissipated. Their ashes are returning to their mended urns and are now magically back in their niches. The "surgeon's" tools have dropped from his flesh and now lie on the floor. Father Demetric is barely hanging on but is determined to take Damian with him. The thirty-three buttons on Father Demetric's cassock fly off, landing on the floor, leaving his garment wide open. A force from within Father Demetric is pulling Damian within him. The survivors run to Damian to help, but to no avail, as he is absorbed into Father Demetric, and together they completely dissipate. Father Demetric's ashes and those of the remaining souls return to the urns and are magically placed back in their niches. All with faceplates restored and intact.

Dr. Lovette, Jeff, and Warren hurry back to the wall, desperately working to get out. Jeff places Dr. Lovette on Warren's shoulders, and at the top of the wall she grabs and pulls at the wet mud until she's able to feel grass.

DR. LOVETTE

I feel grass…it's the ground!

Dr. Lovette continues to pull the mud away until there's a hole big enough for her to crawl through. Warren crawls out next, with Jeff's help. Jeff comes out last with Dr. Lovette and Warren pulling him. They are covered in mud, exhausted, but relieved. It is now morning, and from the distance they can see the construction team with their machines running. They can also see Sebastian, clinging to the column just below the holy tabernacle and they clearly understand the sacrifice he's made.

While on the ground, weak, Dr. Lovette pulls the book from her pocket, and with the book in the air, she commands…

DR. LOVETTE

Turn off those machines!

SCENE 33: ONE MONTH LATER

One month later, Dr. Lovette, Jeff, and Warren return to the church. They are in a solemn mood. They stand on the church grounds and observe a plaque which reads *The Church of All Saints, 1789, Historic Preservation.*

WARREN SYKES

Do you think they knew? The diocese I mean.

DR. LOVETTE

What happened here? Chances are we'll never know the answer to that…no one will.

JEFF MIDTOMAC

Getting anyone to believe our story was impossible. Since Damian's body was not recovered, it was easier for everyone to blame everything that happened down there on him. No one is ever going to admit to knowing what actually occurred down there. As for the physical evidence; the slab, 33 buttocks, furnace an crib and surgical tools, they were never recovered.

WARREN SYKES

To be honest, I'm still having trouble believing it.

JEFF MIDTOMAC

The only positive thing out of this entire nightmare is that they finally accepted that The Church of All Saints is indeed the first Roman Catholic church built in Hudson Valley. And the church won't be closing.

DR. LOVETTE

They plan to conduct tours. The money will subsidize the expenses needed to maintain the upkeep of the church.

Warren has a question that no doubt the other two are also thinking.

WARREN SYKES

Do you think it's really over?

DR. LOVETTE

Well, the wall has been officially consecrated by the bishop and is deemed an official burial site. The book, I've been told, is in a safe undisclosed location, as per the diocese's request. I now know that the battle between good and evil can manifest at any time, place, and… obviously any form. And that the only true weapon against evil is prayer, something obviously Sebastian knew well. To answer your question, is it over…Only God knows.

The three take one last look at the church and walk away.

THE END

EPILOGUE

In a disclosed location, the book *Souls of the Damned* is in a locked, secured room. The book is atop a pedestal, open. A rat crawls on to it, sniffing, scratching, licking. And the book suddenly slams closed. You can see the blood from the rat running down the seams in the book.

ABOUT THE AUTHOR

Angela Dungee-Farley's passion for horror began at the age of eight or nine. As a young girl growing up in Prospect, Virginia, she was unwilling to leave home for any reason if it meant missing her weekly horror shows. As an adult, her passion for horror grew, and one day she decided to write a horror book. *Columbarium: Condemned Souls* is Dungee-Farley's third published horror book. Currently residing in New York, Angela Dungee-Farley is the wife of Dennis Farley and the mother of Daniel Farley.

ABOUT THE BOOK

In 1780, a group of devout Roman Catholics, led by Father Demetric, a missionary priest, migrated from Rome, Italy, to Hudson Valley, New York. But as time passed, Father Demetric took on a new role. He went from religious leader to religious persecutor. He became cruel, calculating, and his punishments...severe. His most heinous deed was denying consecrated ground to those he deemed unworthy. For them, he chose an unconsecrated columbarium wall in the sublevel of the church. It is 225 years later, and the church is for sale. And for eight visitors on a last-minute tour of the church, this night is going to be pure hell. So if you enjoy running, screaming, crying, and praying...read this book.

24800334R00126

Made in the USA
Middletown, DE
07 October 2015